All the Souls

I fechgyn y Mynydd Bach
Ac er cof am
Lowri Gwilym

All the Souls

by

Mary-Ann Constantine

SEREN

Seren is the book imprint of
Poetry Wales Press Ltd
57 Nolton Street, Bridgend, Wales, CF31 3AE
www.serenbooks.com
Facebook: facebook.com/SerenBooks
Twitter: @SerenBooks

ISBN: 978-1-78172-062-2

Typesetting by Elaine Sharples
Printed by Bell and Bain, Glasgow

The publisher works with the financial assistance of
The Welsh Books Council

Contents

The Collectors

Le peuple immense des âmes en peine s'appelle l'Anaon.

The vast population of penitential souls is called the *Anaon*.

Anatole Le Braz, La Légende de la Mort (1902)

Si vous voulez voir des lépreux, hâtez-vous, le dernier ne tardera pas à disparaître en France au moins, avec l'augmentation du bien-être et la propreté individuelle.

If you wish to see lepers, then hurry: it will not be long before the last of them disappears, from France at least, with the rise in living standards and personal hygiene.

Dr P. Aubry, 'La lèpre et les lépreux en Bretagne'
Bulletin de la Société d'Émulation des Côtes-du-Nord (1895)

A village near Plouaret,
Côtes-du-Nord
22 June 1892

Anaon I: Shapes

You will imagine us as bats, or something like. Flittering at dusk, with strange little faces. But it would be best if you think of birds, the tiny brown ones, virtually invisible, that flick at the edges of your vision as you pass a clump of willow or a coppiced ash. Think of a wren in a holly bush, a warbler scuttling down a thick trunk; think, and then, if you can, unimagine the shapes, and remember the movement.

Size varies, as in life, but I have never known anyone bigger than a gull, and she was a rarity, she didn't stay long.

Waiting

He has arranged his best things on the desk like a child, he realises. They are too obvious. So he scatters them artlessly around the study, as a lover would, hoping to reveal himself more slowly, hoping to impress. The Roman coins go in a glass bowl on the broad windowsill; the delicate bronze head on the mantelpiece. A couple of rare editions are shifted to the walnut side table, and the desk is freed up for the business in hand. His annotated copy of Danielsen on top of the photographs and sketches, with Z's letters; a pile of notes to the side. Or should the pictures go on top? He tries it several ways; he cannot think straight. It will be fine, the effect of the room will be fine. Z will be impressed. He goes out through the French windows into the garden for another cigar. He leans against one of the apple trees, furred up with moss and laden with tiny green fruits. Breathing out smoke, he acknowledges the sun, the beautiful yellow light of a June evening that shows his house and garden at their scented, bewitching best. It has been a long afternoon on the longest day of the year.

They watch him waiting, and smile briefly at each other. But his nervousness affects them too, and Madame hustles little Katell back up to the dining room to check the placements again while she tastes the soup and adds a little cream, a little salt. It is delicious. She is sure of that. She knows it would not disgrace a dinner party in Paris, because she worked for his mother for many years in Paris, and was often praised. But she also knows that what is categorically delicious in one country may not be so in another. Who knows what will please this gentleman from the East? Still, they discussed the menu for days and in the end it was his decision. She has done her best.

Katell is so absorbed in the geometry of the dining table – there is something, she feels, not quite right about it – that she does not hear him come in. His sudden voice makes her

12

judder; her face turns pink. He is pleased, however, with the table and pats her benevolently on the shoulder. She waits for a second or two in case there are further orders, prays that she will be able to understand them. But he says nothing else, and so she bobs, and disappears back to the kitchen, leaving him in her place, staring tranced at the three tall unlit candles and the interplay of white and silver. What he remembers has more colour. A deep-blue glaze on a bowl patterned with yellow and red. The pilaff piled into it, coloured and scented and spiced. The pleasure of the faint burning in the throat, like hot sun on skin. Dark faces and eyes of those waiting on, and Z's own slender hands breaking pitta bread, passing it over. Smiling, and talking, and talking.

Z will be at least another hour, but Le Coadic should be getting here by now; his train was due at Plouaret half an hour ago. He heads out again, for the front garden this time, down past the lavender and the roses to the gate.

The click of the latch flusters them until Katell jumps up and sees that it is just the restless doctor leaving. Madame relaxes, lets slip an irreverent proverb in Breton. Katell giggles, goes back to chopping parsley, starts singing.

Anaon II: Twigs

In theory we're supposed to have an Allotted Twig. In practice a certain amount of jostling goes on, especially if a few arrive at once. They do tend to turn up with preconceived ideas about the best spots, the likeliest perches. When you've been here as long as I have you get a certain pleasure from noting just how wrongheaded the new ones can be. I once witnessed a dogfight in a hazel where the resident was actually displaced. The new arrival, a tough little bully, settles on this beautiful straight rod thinking next season's walking stick or broom handle if ever I saw one, and left the resident, whose time was nearly up, all torn and pitiful clinging to a fussy splayed-out twig overhanging the road. What happens then? Nothing at all for three years, three drops in the great eternal ocean, and then one bright morning along comes a little boy with a pocket knife and cuts off the entire overhang to make a roof for his den, so the displaced resident, and several of his companions, are released more or less on time.

Which merely confirms that you cannot cheat the System. Or at least not by trying. I've known plenty get off way ahead of time through the unpredictable behaviour of their nearest and dearest left behind. Complete strangers, too; I've seen him, for example, go out of his way to cut a fly-swat or a letter-opener or a cane for his sweet peas as if permanently driven by pity. On the other hand, I have heard of those who try to plan in advance, as if they were simply making arrangements for their old age: *I'll be in the big ash*, says the matriarch, the fine old ash that practically embraces the farmhouse by now, *so mind you cut it down next year when I'm gone and make furniture, make fenceposts, fix the gate to the marshy field, use the twigs for bedding, burn the rest; mind you do it all within the year.* And the family, more reluctant to lose the old tree than the old woman, do as they're bid, and of course she's anywhere but: probably in a scrubby little hawthorn down the lane,

14

hopping mad. Not, of course, that they know that, so they do have the rewarding glow of filial piety for all their effort. And think of all the others released from such a tree! But best, on balance, not to fight the System, such as it is. You'll do your time.

The splendid straight hazel rod was ignored for another seven years, and then it was only used to prop up the collapsing door of an old outbuilding. Pity, as it would have made a lovely walking stick. Much like his, now.

Arrival

Le Coadic sees the figure at the end of the lane and curses him, mildly, for spoiling the last ten minutes of his walk. He raises his stick in greeting and presses on at a faster pace past the honeysuckle and elderflower, the shocking-pink ragged robin and the darker pink of the foxgloves, past the general tangle of speedwell, nettle, stitchwort, dock. He has observed them all by now in any case, and expects few surprises between here and the house. He has rehearsed their pretty names in French and Breton and rolled half-a-dozen rhyming couplets around his head. Cures and prophylactics, indicators of weather. If any of it worked, he thought vaguely, the people would be bursting with health and good fortune. But it was hard to resist a rhyming couplet. He spent a good half hour last week boiling up eyebright to bathe his tired eyes. He had made her try it too. He thought today they felt a little better, even walking in bright sun. What an evening. And here was the good doctor, almost running, just a little out of breath, to meet him.

'I'm sorry I'm late.' He squeezed the plump hand and lied courteously. 'The train was slow getting into Plouaret.' He had, in fact, spent a quarter of an hour investigating an overgrown spring he had heard about from a friend. The saint had long gone from his, or her, niche, but the friend claimed there was an inscription on the stone above. Le Coadic had pulled off the nettles and brambles, and scraped at the moss with his knife, but had not found the marks conclusive. He washed his hands in the clear water and threw in a little coin for Élise.

'Not at all, *mon ami*, I am so glad you could come at all. How is your wife?'

'Better. She's better. Thank you for asking: she sends her greetings.' He hoped, at some point soon, that he would be able to stop telling lies, that common courtesy and the truth would at least get themselves back on speaking terms. It would be very wearing otherwise. They stuck to the weather, which had been, even for June, quite extraordinary.

'Oh, but this is lovely!' He meant it this time. A family house in stone, with unusually large windows and two old apple trees in the front garden. The doctor was delighted.

'My parents built onto the old farmhouse. We used to come here in the summers from Paris when I was a child. I moved back a few years ago, after they died. I'm here at weekends, mostly; the surgery as you know is at Saint-Brieuc. Too big for me I suppose but it does mean I can receive guests now and again. Let me show you your room; or would you prefer a drink first?'

'Oh, the room please,' said Le Coadic, and let the little man pass.

Katell emerged, smoothing her apron and rubbing flecks of parsley between her finger and thumb.

'Would you show the professor to his room, Katell? You have no other bags?'

'I left the larger one at the station, since we'll be back there tomorrow morning.'

'You travel light, *mon ami*; join me when you're ready.'

Le Coadic smiled and nodded and followed the girl up to a room with a sloping ceiling, overlooking the front garden and the lane.

'Are you from round here?' He spoke to her in Breton and she relaxed immediately, pointing beyond a cluster of trees to a small group of grey buildings.

'That's our farm.'

'Many of you? Brothers and sisters?'

'Six, monsieur, but two of them in the churchyard.' She crossed herself.

He nodded again. 'I like it here,' he said. 'My grandparents came from not far away – I think I may still have relations somewhere near – Guéguen?'

'Blacksmith at Plounevez, monsieur?'

17

'Possibly.'

'He married one of my father's cousins, monsieur.'

'Ah, then we are cousins too. Excellent.'

A loud cough downstairs. Le Coadic looked amused; Katell went pink again, curtsied and vanished. He moved to the little window and let the scent of roses in.

He had thought about having drinks in the library; it would look more professional. But part of him wanted Z to be the first in, so he opted for the garden and was gratified again by Le Coadic's pleasure.

'Honeysuckle,' he raised a glass to his host, 'and those delicious roses. You lucky man.'

'Ah, but you have the sea breezes, my friend. Healthier, more invigorating. I feel quite dreamy, tangled up in all this vegetation.'

They drank peaceably.

'I must thank you properly,' said the doctor, 'for helping me to organise all this.'

'Not at all. Your colleague's work sounds fascinating. I hope the itinerary has given him the opportunities he needed?'

'His last letter was encouraging. Two at Brest, he said, straight off. The hospital, I think. But you were quite right to think of the pardons; and the old colonies. And it is kind of you to come with us.'

'It suits my work too. But tell me how you met him. Was it in Paris?'

For the first time all day, the doctor forgot that he was waiting. He was back in Paris, younger, slimmer, full of ambition and good intentions. The clatter of Z's arrival caught him and threw him like a huge wave breaking. He got to his feet gasping for breath and almost ran round the side of the house to the front gate in time to see his colleague from Constantinople jump neatly down from the carriage and stretch out both his hands with a smile.

'I am late, I am late, ah, my friend, you must forgive me.'

'Oh no no, no no, not late, not late; I really did not expect you till now.'

The bags were unloaded, the driver paid, the carriage clattered off back to Plouaret.

'Please, please come in; no, really. Katell will take the bags.'

'Allow me,' said Le Coadic, who had appeared quietly by the front door. He held out a hand: 'Le Coadic. We have corresponded.'

'Our guide!' said Z with a glorious smile. 'Our Virgil! It is an honour, sir.' They shook hands. He had beautiful hands: long-fingered, manicured, with two big rings. Le Coadic let the two doctors pass him, and went down to the gate.

Madame, he could tell, was getting increasingly uptight. He put off the library again, and after drinks outside in the last of the sunlight they were soon at the white dining table, pulled together by the pooled light of three tall candles and the energy of their conversation. Z's hands danced expressively.

'And the birds,' he was saying. 'Definitely one for you, *mon ami*. Birds with astonishing blue breasts – and we saw them close that day, didn't we? An astonishing blue. They are supposed to be souls, the souls of the damned, never alighting, up and down the Bosphorus, round and round forever.' He smiled. 'Is that not picturesque?'

Aubry nodded. 'That does sound like you, Le Coadic. Is there a Breton parallel?'

'Cruel,' said Le Coadic thoughtfully. 'Here, no, almost the opposite, they perch. For as long as it takes. Though I suspect they are no happier.'

'And when we arrived,' said Aubry, 'at Scutari. And it was so hot I thought I would faint, I remember you said wait for the cemetery, you'll find it chilly enough in there.'

'You did not believe me, *mon ami*.'

'The cypresses are packed so closely, Le Coadic, so black. You cannot imagine how dark it is, how surprising.'

'After all the heat and colour you describe it would be a surprise.'

'Every grave white marble, head and foot, but no sunlight to make it shine. Kilometres and kilometres, dark and cold – I have seen hospitals and morgues all over the western hemisphere but I've never been anywhere more like death.'

Katell came in quietly to remove their soup dishes. Le Coadic thanked her and sent his compliments to the cook. 'I could taste nettles,' he said, 'my mother used to make a soup like that.' Aubry looked embarrassed. 'I'm sorry,' he said, 'but would you mind speaking French? We don't use Breton here, even in the kitchen: the girl's parents asked especially. Till she gets fluent, you know.'

Le Coadic bowed his head in apology. 'Of course,' he said.

'I notice,' said Z smoothly, 'that you people keep your dead closer. I have been to several places now where the graveyard is right in the centre of the village. In fact I saw…'

'Markets held in cemeteries?' said Le Coadic with a smile. 'Fairs? Courting couples? You're right, monsieur. We keep our dead close.'

Z laughed. 'At Rumengol they were making crêpes and mending shoes.'

But Aubry was still in Scutari. 'And those strange turbaned pillars to mark the graves of villains,' he said, 'and the sudden glimpses of the great city over the river, shining in the sun.'

'The dead at Scutari must feel excluded,' said Le Coadic.

'But it's worse for the living,' said Aubry, with some relish at the effect. 'Ah, it is much worse for them, in that crumbling marble mausoleum and it would be even more pitiful were it not for our generous friend here.'

Z looked mildly amused at his colleague's sense of drama.

'My lepers,' he said modestly.

Not trusting Katell, Madame arrived with the duck; the gentlemen applauded.

Anaon III: Three Candles

Teir goulaouen 'bars an ty... He can't not know that, surely? He can't be sitting comfortably at a dinner table with three lighted candles? Why doesn't he say something, or do something, knock his water over, create a diversion? This is not a good beginning, that is the general feeling, he should be more careful.

Some of us however say that it is not his bad luck, it is the little doctor's: his house, his table, his mistake, and that the sudden and violent death which must inevitably result from this oversight will be his concern, not our man's. To which a sizeable portion of the community of souls-in-waiting reply, in an indignant shiver, that the one with the knowledge should always act, it is his responsibility. I feel for the poor man, myself, because the more he knows, and I fear he insists on knowing it all, the harder it will be for him, hemmed in on all sides by the endless dos and don'ts of proper procedure, in all their tedious and conflicting regional variation, until he daren't cross his own threshold for fear of infringing some rule or other. I've known some it gets to like that. They do not walk like other people, for fear of crushing us.

The lack of unanimity is typical, too. If you have ever sat on a rock at the edge of the beach on a sunny day near a clear sea with a light wind you will know what I mean. The sun and the wind reveal the patterns made by small colliding waves, and the effect, very pretty from a distance, is of a rippling net of light, or fishscales, but what is significant is the number of directions involved, as the waves move in and pull back and deflect off the rocks, passing through each other. The knowledge of the anaon, which is, for the record, a very partial and deficient knowledge at best, passes like that from group to group, in clashing ripples, deflected, strengthened, weakened; we call it the gossips. I can already hear the anaon from Bro Leon expressing their scorn; it's four candles, obviously, as anyone knows. Three, confirm the Pays Pourlet, but only if they are in a dead straight line with nothing in between, which is not the case here because of the silver salt cellar, though if anyone reaches for the salt of course it's curtains for someone. The Book, when it comes, we hope, will solve this endless bickering, will nail it once and for all. *Teir goulaouen 'bars an ty / Zo zin pront d'eur maro cry.*

Quest

They were, at last, in the library, with brandy and coffee and petits-fours arranged pleasingly on the small walnut table. He made sure they used the Turkish tea glasses with their bright decorated rims. Le Coadic was brooding like a heron over the map spread out on the far desk. Z prowled gratifyingly around the room, lifting items from sills and shelves, fingering books, nodding, exclaiming, teasing.

'Your Danielsen is in a worse state than mine, *mon ami*. Did you take it to Trondheim?'

'Mm. Look at the notes to Patient D. I saw her, you know. She hung on for me.'

'Lucky man. And this is Morvan's piece?'

'It is. I read it through again after your first letter. Thought I shouldn't let you get away with trampling all over the life's work of a fellow Breton. Matter of honour.'

'But then…?'

'Ah, the truth, *mon ami*. I cannot argue with the truth.'

'Well, we are nearly there. I am pleased with the results so far. They cannot hold out in Paris much longer. I must thank you both again, my dear colleagues, for your superb organisation.'

'Le Coadic is plotting the rest of your itinerary now. Leave it, professor; come and drink your coffee. And you, my friend, give us some account of your first week.'

'In your beautiful country, yes; the greenness is overwhelming. Like being trapped inside the story of the Sleeping Beauty, all the roses and thorns…'

'Not so much in Brest, I imagine,' said Le Coadic, drily, moving over towards the sofa.

'No. But in Brest I was so absorbed, I hardly noticed the place. Can you believe it? My first stop. Straight off the Paris train, two perfect examples, one at the hospital, one at the *dépôt de mendicité*. I recognised them at once – you know that

23

thrill? Like an electric shock. And I'd brought a selection of watercolours from Constantinople so there was no doubt at all. Look, where's my briefcase, I'll show you. I had photographs taken at the hospital. Look at these two hands.'

He passed two pictures round, one a delicate sketch washed with just enough colour to give it depth and form, the other monochrome, pale and ghostly. Both, though, showed a hand bent like a crab; one or two of the fingers, webbed around the roots, had lost their tips; bits of curled fingernail protruded oddly from the stumps.

Z nodded amiably at Aubry: 'That one is Faizal, do you remember? One of the Scutari colony.'

'The rare type B?'

'Yes. He died a few months ago; it accelerated. But the picture is as perfect a type as you could ever hope to see, is it not? And the photograph almost replicates it. That fellow had never left Finistère.'

'Kakouz family?' asked Aubry.

'I didn't think to ask.'

'What was his name?' asked Le Coadic.

'Kokard.'

Le Coadic nodded. 'Could well be, with a name like that. Ropemakers, barrel-makers, some of them still are.'

Aubry clapped his thighs with delight. 'Impressive, very impressive. And after Brest?'

'After Brest,' said Z, 'came the great pardon at Rumengol. Le Coadic's suggestion.' He bowed generously. 'And a very fine one too. Amazing events, your Breton pardons. I was several times quite distracted from my task.'

'Saint-Jean will be even bigger,' said Le Coadic cheerfully. 'Did you get the ferry to Le Faou?'

'Packed!' The eyebrows and the hands went up together. 'We could hardly move. Five in the morning and the light across the bay was so subtle, so dreamlike, my friends, I shall never forget it. And all the *paysans* dressed up and crammed in: I saw several more deformed hands, and would have examined them too but we could barely move our own arms. It can't be safe to pack them in like that. There must be accidents, shipwrecks.'

'There are.' Le Coadic got up and went over to the window. A handful of white moths were trying desperately to get in. He felt a ripple of disquiet.

'And at Rumengol?' asked Aubry, expectantly. Z almost purred.

'An ulcerous type.'

'You're sure?'

'Quite, quite sure. I told you we were nearly there. We shall have the full range by the time the week is out, every possible type and combination, at every possible stage. They will have to accept it.'

Aubry poured brandy into three coloured glasses and raised one towards the chandelier: 'To Truth, my friends! To Truth.'

Le Coadic was recalling the pink doll cheeks and bright blue eyes of Our Lady of Rumengol, hoisted onto shoulders, carried on a wave of solemn singing. He put his coffee cup down very carefully on the windowsill and turned round. 'Let me show you the route to Saint-Jean,' he said.

Anaon IV: Trains

Trains. When I came over there were no such things, but they did not surprise me at all. That has a lot to do with the way we perceive time and what we see in it. Desperately erratic; it comes in pulses, sometimes pulled into a pinpoint where all is pure present – your sinful self, your twig, the waiting, and every single moment in the wind and the rain experienced minute by minute to the full, hours after days after weeks after months after years, and you know that you are getting your penance well and truly done as it should be, cold and miserable and grimly sequential, no cutting corners. Then at other times it opens out hugely like a frightening umbrella, and you are hovering over the centre of a vast lake of time with the past and the future lapping round the edges, so that you get a sense, somewhat blurry, of what has been and what is to come. It makes you feel very sick at first, your mind spins horribly. I thought at the beginning that it was part of the punishment, but I prefer to think of it now more as compensation for the long stints perching. A penitential perk.

So yes, trains, I could see them coming, as it were. I even thought briefly they might get me off early, with such a frantic clearing of scrubland and forest for the new tracks, but, realistically, even at the height of the nation's passion for public transport, my little patch was never going to be on the way to anywhere. And there are some, even round here, who believe that clearance isn't good enough; it's not precise enough, it doesn't count as 'tools', and that those whose trees and bushes are merely destroyed in the name of progress simply move on, dispossessed, to cluster in the next available place. I say to them sod that, bring on the machines: I believe they are released.

And I have seen, close now, really quite close, a time when thousands of us anaon will come home on these very trains, clinging pathetically to knapsacks, perched on exhausted uniformed shoulders. Thousands. Cursing the day they were born Breton and compelled to trek home across the breadth of bleeding France in the company of the wounded to find their bespoke perches. I cannot think that they will have to spend long on their twigs, poor buggers, poor children, after what they have already done out there. Even taking into account original sin and the inherent naughtiness of small boys, some of these lads, including his, should be in credit.

Morlaix

They were on the early train from Plouaret to Morlaix. Morning sun had already greened the little hedged-in fields; cows had been milked and shifted from the courtyards to the pasture; their muddy tracks were, unusually, dried hard. It will begin to feel normal, this weather, thought Le Coadic; soon it will begin to feel like a right, not a blessing. I hope it can last till the Saint Jean. He took out his notebook and began to jot down ideas.

Aubry was absorbed in an article his colleague had given him, but Z watched Le Coadic with interest.

'You research as we do, among the poor and the sick,' he observed.

'Indeed.'

'And this excursion will also be part of your research?'

'Yes.'

'Tell me. I find it all fascinating.'

Le Coadic closed his book. 'I'm really interested,' he said, 'in popular beliefs about death, about the afterlife: ghosts and premonitions and what happens to souls after passing. I've been collecting them since I was at college, and one day they will go into a book, or several. But for these next few weeks I'm specifically employed by the Ministry of Culture to collect traditions about local saints. I have barely started. There's a lot of ground to cover. Literally.' He waved his hand expansively towards the peaceful world outside the carriage window. 'There are hundreds of them. Hundreds. Tiny local saints, virtually unknown outside their parish, beyond the square mile around their well, their rock, their little chapel. We tend to have a name, a site, and not much more: occasionally there's a bit of legend or a saying. That is what I'm after.' He looked out of the window again, and added, 'St John is different of course, but not a bad place to start.'

'Different because he's not local?'

Le Coadic smiled. 'We make all our saints local, one way or the other. But you're right. From a scientific point of view it is much richer, more complex; there's more to compare it with, right across Europe. Beyond. I expect you know the sort of thing.'

They watched more cows and barns and fields slide past, and, for a while, followed a little river overhung with willows. Then Le Coadic added, almost to himself. 'The poor and the sick do it better than the rest of us, I suppose.' Then he looked at Z. 'Are you never afraid of being infected, working with your lepers?'

'Another myth,' said the doctor calmly. 'Not infectious. And, as for the rest, I use plenty of soap.' He smiled again, with a trace of mischief, 'And yourself?'

They had a late and luxurious breakfast in the Grand Café at Morlaix, under the soaring arches of the viaduct that had brought them in. Z was ebullient, elated by the viaduct and the shamelessly Parisian style of the café, which made him, he said, nostalgic for his student days. They watched the market in progress in the square, laughed at the English tourists buying baskets and cheap lace. After a while Le Coadic excused himself and went off to the Imprimerie Lédan to see what new pieces he was printing. 'It's mostly terrible stuff,' he said, 'all dismal *cantiques* and street ballads, but I have found the odd gem.' They arranged to meet later, at the surgery of Dr Proulx.

Z and Aubry walked down to the port and contemplated the busy boats arriving and unloading alongside the tobacco factory.

'I am a patriotic smoker,' said Aubry. 'Morlaix cigars are very fine. Do have one.'

Z was lazily eyeing up a small group of workers, mostly older women, waiting for their shift, chewing tobacco.

'Leave it,' said Aubry. 'Come and walk up the river with me for half an hour. You'll have enough to look at later on.'

They walked along the bank, past the bright sails of jostling boats, the sun warm on their dark tailored coats, their white shirts tight around the chest and neck. Not far up the water opened out, became bluer, saltier; there were gulls. A few tasteful large houses clung to the wooded slopes for effect. But the two men were back in Paris, swapping opinions of erstwhile colleagues. 'I have convinced Villiers,' said Z, 'although he asked me to keep his revised opinion secret.' He pulled a letter from his breast pocket: '*Courage et succès,* he says here. But they cling, *mon ami.* They are desperate not to believe me.'

'I think that Morvan himself would be convinced, if the poor man were still alive. What more can you do?'

He laughed softly. 'They want to isolate a bacillus; I have told them there is no point, it could never be conclusive, not with this one. It's like a rainbow: a spectrum of symptoms. You know that.'

Swallows dived and flicked up again ahead of them. They turned back towards the town.

'But there'd be no harm, I suppose, in sending a specimen if you found one? For them to try?'

'None at all. I imagine they wouldn't believe any more or any less.'

'It's a possibility, then. Do you want to try the morgue?'

'Let's see what Proulx has to offer first. Perhaps then, yes, later, if there's time.'

Dr Proulx's surgery was in the *quartier* Saint-Melaine, still known as the Madeleine, on the north slope of the town; it was all steps and alleys, houses and terraces packed in a picturesque jumble into tiny streets. Le Coadic found it tucked behind the tall spire of the church, a narrow house that opened up surprisingly once you were inside. In the waiting room he passed a bundled female figure in black, apparently asleep; he inclined his head and murmured a greeting, but she didn't stir.

Inside the consulting room he found the three medical men at a large table, facing a man of about fifty. He was small and thin and terrified. Both his hands were flat on the surface in front of him; his face was pocked and covered in boils.

'I still say type B,' said Aubry, defensively, looking to Z for support.

'Syphilis,' said the Morlaix doctor through his beard. 'Syphilis.'

Z put the tips of his fingers together and raised his black eyebrows.

'Ah,' he said. 'This one is difficult. But I think Proulx is right this time. Syphilis. Which makes it, I think, one each?' He dropped a coin in front of the frightened man, who grabbed it swiftly and fled the room. Aubry, to hide his embarrassment, greeted Le Coadic with gratuitous warmth.

'Come on in, *mon cher ami*. We need a translator. We'll get a better diagnosis with a proper translator to hand.'

'Surely Doctor Proulx…' replied Le Coadic tactfully. But Proulx, a man of few words in any language, merely shrugged, and waved him in.

'La Madeleine not as productive as you'd hoped?' said Le Coadic cheerily, finding himself a place. 'And you, doctor, you have yet to be won over by our learned colleagues here?'

'On the contrary, *mon ami*,' put in Z swiftly. 'Proulx is one of us; indeed, he was a most helpful correspondent in the months before I came over. And I do believe,' the eyebrows arched again, 'that he has saved the best till last.'

Proulx stood up and bowed stiffly, then went through to the waiting room. There was a minute or so of noise, of rustling and coughing, and then he reappeared, ushering before him a large woman in a worn and patched black dress.

A delicate white lace coiffe framed what was left of her face; one of her claws held a little wooden crucifix on a leather thong. She looked placidly at the three men seated at the huge table before her, and did not appear surprised when all three, as if hauled up suddenly on strings, stood and bowed. Dr Proulx pulled the previous patient's chair out for her and went to join the others.

There was a brief silence as the men and the woman with the monstrous face looked at each other across the table, and then Z spoke.

'Madame,' he said, 'it is an honour to meet you.'

The expression did not change, although the eyes looked at him thoughtfully.

'My colleagues and I,' he continued, 'would be grateful for the opportunity to examine you more closely; to draw up a thorough description of your...' he paused, 'your affliction. We do not wish to frighten you or to harm you in any way, and what is more,' he pulled three bright coins from a pocket and placed them in a row in front of him, 'we are willing to pay you for your time.'

The eyes rested a moment on the coins; then turned back to Z.

'Le Coadic,' he said quietly. 'Will you translate?'

In the exchange that followed, the woman's expression altered very little, although her eyes brightened and she waved an arm. Her voice rasped like old wood. It became clear there was a problem.

'She says,' said Le Coadic, glancing at Proulx who must have understood but had shown no signs of following, 'she says that she can't stay long. She has to leave very soon to get to Sant Yann, to Saint Jean, by tomorrow afternoon. Walking, that is. She's a beggar. She can't afford to miss it, even for twice that much.' He nodded at the coins. 'I've told her we're going too; I said we could take her. I'm confident that if you promise to get her there in good time for the procession she'll stay.'

'Madame,' said Z, looking very earnest, 'I promise, I give you my word, that you will not miss the Sant Yann.'

'*Bennos Doue,*' said the woman, and crossed herself with a claw.

Z came to life, and began effortlessly ordering events. 'Proulx: equipment. I want clean needles, a candle, surgical spirit, cloth. Do you have ice? No? Who has ice? Fishsellers; restaurants: Aubry, find me a small box of ice, then you will come and take notes. Le Coadic, you find out where she's from, where she's been; when the disease began, whether it is in her family, while I do a preliminary sketch. Ask her to put her hands on the table.'

He took out a pad of white paper and began to sketch quickly, deftly, humming under his breath and throwing questions at Le Coadic. Aubry returned with the ice and fussed around for a minute; then he too pulled out clean white paper from his briefcase and sat down. He held his pen like a dog waiting to be taken for a walk.

'We'll begin at the top,' said Z, nodding to Aubry. 'Ready, Proulx? Keep her talking, Le Coadic, it will be easier for everyone; tell me anything useful as we go along.'

Le Coadic and the woman had in any case kept up a quiet undertow of Breton. Z moved closer. She did not blink.

'She's called Tilly, Marie-Josèphe Tilly; fifty or thereabouts, born and brought up here in the Madeleine. Father made barrels.'

'Hair,' said Z. 'What I can see of it reasonably well preserved. Eyebrows, on the other hand, non-existent.'

'She isn't exactly a beggar; more a pilgrim.'

'Face largely paralysed; gashed with scars, most healed over but two or three open; tubercles in the thicker folds of skin.'

'A pilgrim-by-proxy. She does penitential journeys on behalf of other people.'

'Left cheek: an ulcer about two centimetres long and half a centimetre wide; part of the nose – pardon me, Madame – destroyed from within by another ulcer.'

'Which is why she has to go to the Sant Yann; she has business there. Travels a lot, obviously, mostly Tregor, northern Cornouaille; occasionally Leon.'

'The nose is seriously deformed in any case, flattened. Nodules, some quite large, between the eyebrows and on earlobes. Chin appears puffed and swollen. Voice very husky; considerable damage to the voicebox.'

'Her mother still lives in the Madeleine; father died ten years ago in a cart accident.'

'Arms. Could you ask her to roll up the sleeves a little? Ah, thank you.'

'The disease began about twenty-five years ago. It is God's punishment for vanity.'

'Upper arm: pigmented areas alternating with ulcerated patches. Please note especially large ulcer on the right arm almost circular in shape, depressed, as if branded by a disc.'

'She was beautiful. But God and the blessed Virgin saw her soul was in mortal danger.'

'And another, approximately four centimetres by three centimetres on the back of the wrist – sorry, that's still the right wrist – suppurating.'

'She found a small lump on her forehead. She tried everything to get rid of it. And then one day she washed her face in holy water from the church, and the lumps began to spread.'

'Wrist area on left hand full of nodules. Both hands clawlike, almost rigid. The index of the right hand appears severely damaged; possibly infected.'

He lingered, and caught Aubry's glance, and said it again, slowly. 'Possibly infected.'

Then he stood back from her a moment and nodded to Proulx. 'Vision first, then sensation.' Proulx slipped white gloves on and moved behind her. He blocked each eye in turn as Z held up fingers, a lighted candle, a pencil.

'Left eye almost blind, I'd say. You can see the discoloration to the cornea. More vision in the right. Now for the needles.

Le Coadic, do explain to her how necessary all this is; it shouldn't hurt much. Can you make her say yes each time she feels anything at all? Good. Aubry, are you ready?'

He held the long needle expertly in his slim hands, and focused only on each patch of skin. Aubry drew a rough doll's head divided into six sections, and then two flat hands, and began to map the woman's yelps with neat little crosses. When they were done whole patches of the doll's face were still blank, and the hands were almost completely clear. He shook his head in wonder and held the paper up for Z to see.

'Amazing,' he said. 'It is amazing.'

'But I, my friend, am not amazed.' He held his hand out for the paper with a look so tender Aubry almost blushed.

Marie-Job sat with her hands on the table, her lips moving, her eyes closed, apparently praying. Le Coadic left her to it and went to join the others.

'That's all now, isn't it?'

Z put a gentle hand on his arm. 'Ah, *mon ami*, I think we will still need your help.'

They helped her back into the waiting room and Proulx found a servant from his own house to bring her coffee and bread and tobacco. They shut the door and sat back around the table. Z cleared his throat and gestured towards the pile of notes and sketches: 'Proof,' he said. 'Proof to convince the most sceptical. I'm grateful, more than I can say, to all of you, my colleagues, for making this happen. With this I could go back to Paris tomorrow, fully armed, and vanquish every last unbeliever.'

He sat for a moment, but they knew there would be more.

'But that, I think, would be wrong. My Hippocratic oath, after all, requires that I do everything in my power to help our patients wherever they are, and wherever I find myself, as quickly and efficiently as possible. Is that not so?'

No one denied it. He turned to Le Coadic.

'What my colleagues here have realised, and you perhaps have yet to do, is that our patient has a serious infection in the index finger of her right hand. It is not unusual in these cases; because they cannot feel pain, cuts, even serious wounds, may go unnoticed, they can become infected. I know that I do not need to convince my colleagues here that immediate removal of the finger will prevent the infection from spreading and almost certainly save her life. The disease, of course, will kill her eventually in other ways, but there is no reason why she should die in the next few months. As, I believe, she most certainly will if we do not operate as soon as possible. To minimise her distress, I think we should do it at once.'

Le Coadic raised his head as if to speak but Z was in full flow.

'I have done this before. I did it a few weeks ago in Constantinople. And the most miraculous thing is that our patient will feel no pain.'

Le Coadic briefly raised both hands, but did not say anything.

'If you, *mon ami*, can talk to her while we operate, keep her thoughts distracted, keep her calm, it will all go so quickly she will not know it has happened. Remember, we are saving her life, and she will feel no pain. Do we all agree?'

They all agreed.

Anaon V: Taxonomies

We're all desperate to be in the Book, of course, even those who led exemplary lives, giving to the poor and praying a lot and working their socks off, and who now find themselves on unremarkable twigs with no added extras, for an unremarkable length of time, in moderate temperatures, waiting rather smugly to go to heaven. Very little narrative life in *them*, I feel. Now a poor sinner like myself, five hundred years and counting in an oak that refuses to die a natural death, struck by lightning, hollowed and twisted, no good now for beams or planks and so far off the beaten that you'd need a real effort of will to get the tools out here to do the job. An excellent case study, if he only knew, what with my sins being so many, so unusual and so apt.

There is endless speculation about his taxonomy. Something sternly Linnaean would work best, I am convinced of that, a proper natural history of the species and habitats of the anaon, carefully teasing out their similarities and differences. The drowned, for example, if it is not tactless of me to dwell on them, should be separated out into:

The drowned at sea
– working, as sailors or fishermen
– travelling, to pardons or for pleasure, as his own beloved sisters and their husbands and his father will be one day
– and those who are occasionally swept – or throw themselves – off cliffs and promenades

The drowned in rivers
– working, as fishermen, or bargemen, or loaders of tobacco and sardines at the docks
– travelling, to pardons, or for pleasure, or both
– fooling around

All the Souls

The drowned in ponds, wells or ditches
- children
- drunkards
- suicides
- the murdered, especially newborns, you'd be surprised how many.

And then, for each type of drowning, the relevant premonition:

- by dream, witness the story of the parents obliged to watch their little girl asleep, unable to wake, dreaming that her bed, and then the whole room, was filling slowly with water.
- by signs, subtle and deadly: a false reflection; white moths outside a window.
- less subtly, an encounter with wet and ragged Iannik an Aod who, when their time is coming, calls out in a fearful voice to those who live and work along the coast.

And then, for each type of drowned soul, the most likely place of penance: not always twigs, from what I hear, though many of course end up in gorse bushes and thorn trees along the coast. Witness the admittedly aberrant case of the woman who did fifty years in a farmyard water tank, waiting for someone to throw in a 'rescue pebble' (not a concept I would, myself, have permitted in the great scheme of things, but there you are, recorded is recorded and it must be classified somehow). Which some child did, eventually, and was startled out of his wits to see it thrown back out again.

And then, if necessary, any significant regional variation: assuming, as they all seem to, that Tregor will be taken as the norm, the gold standard, the Attica of Breton tradition.

And that, heaven help us, is just the drowned.

I'm no expert, of course, having only ever destroyed books, not written them, but I suspect, deep down, that his weakness for sentimental description will get in the way of him producing a decent working system. Though I keep that thought, as far as I can keep anything now, to myself.

Finger

Half an hour later Le Coadic found himself sitting on the left hand side of Marie-Job, talking to her about songs. Aubry and Z had strapped her right forearm to a heavy wooden block. The claw-hand refused to flatten, so they had allowed the fingers to curl over the end of the block in such a way as to allow the base of the index to be pushed down firmly against the wood. The knives were laid out ready and there were clean white cotton squares and boiling water to hand. Proulx positioned himself behind her, ready to hold her still if need be.

'Shall we sing something now?' suggested Le Coadic with panic in his voice. 'A cantique? Something to the Virgin?'

'*Gwerz Sant Yann*,' she rasped.

'Of course. Come on then.' And he began, in his low soft tenor, to intone the dirge-like hymn to St John traditionally sung during the procession of the banners. Mari-Jobig's hoarse voice joined in. Le Coadic was trying so hard not to look at the doctors moving towards the knives that he was well into his second stanza before he realised that the voice next to him was singing a different song. Without quite stopping his own, but dropping it to a compliant murmur, he started listening to the words, getting clearer now as she found her rhythm. As the two men in front of him exchanged low monosyllables a slow revelation dawned; his heart fluttered and he began searching his pockets for his notebook and pencil. He put a hand on her near arm.

'Please, Mari-Jobig, begin it again.'

She began it again, rocking slightly as she sang and, wisely he felt, keeping her eyes closed, while he deftly jotted down the slow couplets and memorised the tune, joining her on the repeated second line, nodding and nodding his head in quiet delight. The song unrolled gradually in his notebook; a unicorn of a song, a beauty: the legend of the holy finger of Sant Yann distilled into Breton couplets.

The brave young soldier weeps; he is fighting the English in Normandy. He weeps for his native parish, Traon Meriadek.

The doctors continued to exchange comments in a low undertone, but the rasping voice now filled the room.

He only stops weeping when he kneels to pray in the local church, before the holy relic: the finger of St John the Baptist. Rescued from the infidel by the martyred Saint Tecla, the relic fills him with a curious joy. Gradually his longing for home is subsumed into a longing for the presence of the sacred finger.

Le Coadic gently unrolls the song on the white page, and sings with her, head down, he cannot see the knives.

But now the wicked English are vanquished. The soldier can go home. He goes one last time to the church, and weeps again; now he does not want to leave. He prays himself senseless. When he revives, he gets to his feet and turns himself west.

'The trees,' croaks Mari-Jobig, 'even the tallest ashes, they bow down to him on the road.'

The doctors have clustered around the hand; she stares blankly ahead. She sees the brave young Breton reach the top of his village, walking full of joy like a man in seven-league boots, the little birds singing him in and the sun sparkling on the sea.

'Where he rests,' she rasps, 'where he rests, a spring bursts out from the ground.'

There is an awful noise. Z reaches for the cotton squares.

And when he arrives at the chapel the candles all light of their own accord and the bell rings and the people come running.

Z turns to them both with triumphant eyes and an expansive smile, but before he can speak Le Coadic has hushed him with a fierce gesture.

'Wait. Give me two more minutes. Please, go away.'

The eyebrows raise, the doctor bows, and backs off.

And when they come running, the people, they find the young man kneeling at the altar, his arms outstretched, radiant with joy.

Z leaves the room; Aubry adjusts the dressing and unbuckles the arm.

And holy Sant Yann has permitted the miracle to happen. His finger leaps from the soldier's flesh, onto the altar. Hidden in his wrist, between flesh and bone. It leaps like a salmon to its new home. Holy Sant Yann be praised.

'Amen,' says Le Coadic. 'Amen.'

Then he stands abruptly, scraping his chair, and rushes outside to the evening sun.

They had sent her back to her mother's for the night, and arranged to have a meal taken round for them both. Proulx had gone home and now Z, Aubry and Le Coadic sat outside under a plane tree at a pleasant restaurant in one of the squares. Swifts dipped around them; pigeons cooed in the higher branches of the tree.

'No,' said Aubry very firmly.

'But she wants it.'

'So do we.'

'But it's hers.' Le Coadic looked rather shaken.

Z put his fingertips together and closed his eyes.

'Why does she want it?' he said diplomatically.

'For Sant Yann. To dedicate it or something ghastly. It's important.'

'And why do we want it?' he looked fondly at Aubry.

'For Paris. Proof. It is more important.'

'Perhaps.'

Le Coadic began to get agitated.

'You can't…' he began, but Z cut him short.

'We can, *mon ami*; we could. I suspect it really will make a difference to those fools in the Salpêtrière. I can't let you just walk off with it after all the trouble we've been to. But I should think we can reach an agreement, a compromise.'

Le Coadic shrugged and reached for his wine. 'We will come with you tomorrow, as planned. I am curious to see this festival before I go, in any case. She can have it – under extremely strict conditions – to dedicate to her gods or whatever tomorrow evening, and the following day I carry on to Paris – as planned. *Et voilà* – science and religion are satisfied. What do you say to that?'

He raised his glass and smiled at them both. They raised theirs.

Anaon VI: Roads

And roads. You will not believe this but the roar and clatter of trains is as nothing, I tell you, as nothing, to what is coming our way. The matted muddy lanes, wheel-loosening, splattering, splintering lanes, what a relief, you will say, to see them smoothed out, smartly surfaced, flat as flagstones, what a pleasure to be alive and bowling along in the trap to the clean pleasant noise of clopping, as they will be shortly on the relatively decent and well-travelled road to Sant Yann. But it won't be horses for much longer. When the roads come, according to a popular prophecy much in vogue in the middle ages and still doing the rounds in some areas, then will come Trouble and Despair and War. And if the prophetic mode seems melodramatic and not a little imprecise, I can tell you for free, having glimpsed it myself, that in Morlaix alone they will pave over the very river to find room for the bright massed ranks of cars.

And that's not all. At first, what a carnage of trees, what an orgy of release: heaven and the other place struggling to cope with the overflow, the technically liberated anaon clustered miserably at the pearly and the not-so-pearly gates like camps full of refugees waiting to be processed. But then, concrete. Rivers of concrete, setting fast, from the little slow meandering ones that will take English visitors from calvary to calvary and from boulangerie to patisserie through all the neat, geraniumed villages of the coastal belt, to the rush of the double *voie-express* linking the busy towns. Brest will rise from the ashes in concrete. Villages will give their hearts to it. And in one tiny place in Finistère the municipality will, quite suddenly, realise that it is down to its last *talus*, its last traditional banked and planted hedge, and the hedge will be labelled and protected and deemed a rare and valuable thing. But what then for the poor anaon stranded in its beautiful old beech? Cut off from the immensity by concrete; and not only them. Anaon stuck on idiotic roundabouts planted with hydrangeas. Anaon islanded by slipways. Trapped between traffic lanes flowing north and south. The gossips, never desperately reliable, hitting more and more patches of emptiness, with nothing to ripple through; strips of concrete entirely devoid of souls.

Saint-Jean-du-Doigt

The following morning Aubry organised the hire of a coach and they set off north for the coast. He had persuaded Z to sit with him outside, partly to appreciate the beauties of the Breton countryside in the continued unnatural brilliance of the sun; partly to escape the smell of Mari-Jobig sweating imperturbably in her black dress. As the fields and hedges rolled past they talked intensely of medical matters, and Aubry's heart flashed and swam with pleasure like a goldfish in clear water. Le Coadic, who much preferred the outside, dealt with a nauseous, if faint, sense of guilt by courteously keeping her company. After some preliminary conversation he suggested they go through the song again; he noted variations and added a couple of newly remembered verses. Her father sang it, she said; she did not know where he had got it from. Had she ever read *Le Grand*? he asked. She could not read, she said. And, she added, before he could ask, nor could he, her father. After a while she closed her eyes and began to snore. He turned a page and sketched her, a benign, almost queenly figure, jotting down adjectives and phrases in French and Breton until she had a fuzzy halo of words around her head. And as he worked, the sense of his next book dawned pleasurably upon him. It would be a literary pilgrimage to different religious sites, with this extraordinary woman, this pilgrim by proxy, linking them. Into the vivid descriptions of local life for which he was rapidly becoming noted he could weave the tragic stories of people who paid her their few sous to undertake these penitential journeys on their behalf. A woman so ravaged she seemed to be of another species altogether, taking on the sins of others. But a dead cert for salvation, he thought, once she made it over the other side.

Beside him on the seat lay a small wooden box lined with sterilised white cotton on which lay the crooked finger.

The Collectors

The coach rattled into the square at Saint-Jean-du-Doigt and Z jumped down and opened the door with an exaggerated bow. '*Monsieur,*' he said, '*Madame, nous sommes arrivés.*' Le Coadic unfolded his long legs and stepped down into the sunshine with relief. Elated by his new idea, he felt disposed to be charming.

'And how was our incomparable Breton countryside for you, doctor? I imagine you hardly noticed it, the pair of you; you medical men have no appreciation of beauty.'

In her dark corner Mari-Jobig opened blurred eyes and saw only brightness and indeterminate figures; they were laughing loudly. She crossed herself and began to pray. Then Z leaned in towards her and plucked the wooden box from the seat.

'Madame,' he said, 'Come. You see, as I promised, you have reached Sant Yann.'

Le Coadic thought he could smell the sea and sense it in the quality of the light up ahead, but it was muffled by the noise and smells of the holidaying crowd. There were stalls around the square selling crèpes and sausages and coffee; others were piled with gifts and votive offerings, little bunches of dried herbs. Mari-Jobig, disoriented at not arriving on foot, stood for a long moment blinking in the square. Then she looked around for Le Coadic and nodded her head in the direction of the church.

'*An Aotrou Yann,*' she said.

'*Ya,*' said Le Coadic. '*Deuet omp.*'

'*Ha ma biz?*'

'The Doctor has it safe in the box. When would you like to dedicate it?'

She looked thoughtful. The sun glared down fiercely from directly overhead.

Later, she said. With the procession and the *tantad*. She waved her stick at the massive construction of wood and furze piled up like an enormous hedgehog near the churchyard wall. 'I'll do my work first.'

'May we keep it safe for you until then?' He spoke gently, but held his breath.

She shrugged. '*Mad eo.*'

He breathed out. 'Good. We will meet you here by the hotel when the procession reaches the fountain.'

The three men went into the hotel overlooking the square to find their rooms and have lunch. Mari-Jobig headed purposefully towards the church to fulfil her various tasks as pilgrim by proxy for half-a-dozen clients who, on their deathbeds or in childbed or detained by something less pressing, had been unable to attend the pardon for themselves. She would circle the church and pray for them, for their loved ones, she would light candles with the money they had given her; there were several orders too for bunches of the powerful herbs, which she acquired from a particular stallholder with whom she had a business agreement. She waved her wounded hand at him proudly. 'It was a miracle,' she told him with a twisted grin, 'a miracle of Sant Yann; when the knife came, I felt no pain.' Then she stuffed the bundles into the brown bag slung round her shoulders and went off to find something to eat from a woman she knew at another stall.

Le Coadic left the others to coffee and cake. Z was visibly relaxing, slowing down, satisfied that he had seen and done enough. He would wander out later to browse the crowd but without the same predatory hunger as before; for the next hour, he would be warm and entertaining, fuelling Aubry's adoration on this their last day together for the months, possibly years ahead. Aubry was telling him about the lecture he had planned for the Société Archéologique des Côtes-du-Nord, an excellent opportunity to spread the word about Z's discovery to a wider audience, to a group of enlightened men who were not all obsessed with defending the honour of their precious *maladie de Morvan*.

'A splendid idea, *mon ami*. As soon as I get to Paris I shall send you copies of my notes.'

Aubry extended a plump arm over the coffee table with a box of Morlaix cigars. Z delicately extracted one, lit it, and blew smoke upwards. Then he put the cigar down on an ashtray still smoking, picked up the other little wooden box from the glass table in front of him and opened it. He sat in quiet, heavy-lidded contemplation; Aubry rose from his armchair and padded round to look over his shoulder. But his view of the finger lying curled on its white cotton square was disturbed by a rush of tenderness brought on by the sight of the tiny flecks of grey in the curls at the nape of his master's neck.

Le Coadic was now the hunter, moving through the crowds, his senses heightened by a quiet excitement collecting deep inside. He picked them out for his vignettes, a pretty courting couple sat in peaceful silence on the churchyard wall; the blind man selling Lédan's ballad sheets, mostly religious, but occasionally more sensational, bawling out verses at the top of his terrible voice. A one-legged beggar on crutches so festooned with rags he looked like a wishing tree, a barbarian chief. This, he decided, was the festival of the beggar, of the lowest life of all; he rejoiced in it. It was like drinking red wine for him, this feeling he had; he would be their poet, their interpreter, he would dignify them with clouds of golden words. He would dedicate his life to recording, celebrating, the poverty and religiosity that were the two faces of his country's soul.

The sun was too hot. The smell of frying pork was tinged bizarrely with other smells: the pines from the coast, the sweet, sickly scent of yellow broom. It was Mari-Jobig he wanted. Where was she? He put his notebook away again to push more effectively through the black dresses and white lace coiffes, the large brimmed hats, the smell of sweat, the laughter.

He found her squatting in the precinct of the churchyard, her back up against the low stone wall, chewing tobacco and counting coins awkwardly into a leather pouch. He hung back out of sight and watched her getting used to her bound and mutilated hand. Not that the remaining fingers were very much use, he thought, all bent like that, all rigid. When she had finished counting she sat back and closed her eyes; he watched her lips move. After a while she seemed to go to sleep, so Le Coadic made himself comfortable on a grave slab and retrieved his notebook for another sketch. It would help him find the words later.

Anaon VII: Cold

Cold. If I were to count the ways we would be here for ever; and I, at any rate, am not banking on that, surely after five hundred years I must be coming up for release, wrong though I was to do what I did. But I can give you some idea, from the sheer cut of the wind at the very tips of the bare trees, to the dark black waters of the bog. It is usually a wet cold, a damp cold, a depressing grey blanket of cold, very rarely modulating to ice and snow, but nothing arctic, nothing dramatic, no crackling crystals forming in the breath, no fingers of deathly frost burning the skin. The days when the rime fastens us to the little twigs are difficult ones for us of course, and when the sidelong rain at the top of your tree turns to hail it is naturally not too pleasant, but it is more the never being warm that makes us so despairing, that and the gap between us and the living, so much worse in spring and summer and as everyone keeps saying, *ma doue,* what a summer this is. To be stuck shivering in a permanent November and look out over Brittany this hot, hot June adds a nice twist to any penance, do you not think.

But God and the Blessed Virgin in their infinite pity, which is, I suspect, more hers than his, have ordained that there shall be two days of very brief respite, when the freezing souls may gather round a decent fire and gain a little benefit. All Souls, our big day, is a way off yet but the summer St John is also ours and we watch the preparations with some interest, the villages competing to make the biggest pile, the households saving a little here and there, the children collecting gorse stubs, the groups of roaming lads off after dark nicking their neighbours' stash. Oh yes we are excited now, there is no denying it, at the thought of those red flames, those burning hot stones.

Fire

The three men watched from the balcony, impressed, as the huge swaying banners came down the hills from two directions. The young men carrying them under the burning sun were red-faced with strain, deadly serious. The crowd chanted prayers to keep them going, to keep them up. Sometimes they dipped with the strain of it. As they approached the square various other groups from neighbouring villages, some come in little flotillas along the coast, carrying their own saints, their own banners, merged with the other crowds and fell in step with the procession. A group of dressed-up children led a lamb, also dressed up, around the church; the priest pronounced blessings. The bell in the tall spire began to toll for vespers. At this sound everyone surged around the enormous spiky mass of the bonfire, which was now festooned with bits of ribbon and flowers. A thin wire stretched diagonally upwards from the very top of the mound across the graveyard to the church tower.

'We have the best view up here,' said Aubry, comfortably. 'It's quite a spectacle.'

'The best place for the procession,' agreed Le Coadic, 'but for the fire you need to be with the crowd. Besides, we have to find Mari-Jobig. She wants her... she wants to do the dedication soon, I think.'

'The fire will be much better from here,' said Aubry. 'I'm staying.' He gestured to the bottle of wine on a small table beside him and directed a faintly pleading look towards Z, who smiled at them both, and patted the pocket with the small wooden box. 'I'll come down with you now and find our companion,' he said cheerfully, 'but I agree with Aubry: the effect will be truly spectacular from up here. I'll be back, my friend, as soon as Sant Yann has blessed our little offering, to help you with that bottle and watch the rest from the gods.'

The Collectors

She was waiting for them just outside the entrance; her stiff face turned to greet them, imperturbable as ever. She held out her mutilated hand like a beggar for coins: '*Ma biz.*'

Z reached into his pocket and drew out the box. He held it in front of her and became suddenly very serious.

'Tell Marie-Josèphe,' he said, looking straight at her. 'Tell her that what lies in this box is precious to people in places far beyond Breiz-Izel, far even beyond the big hospitals and the doctors in Paris. Tell her that in the Holy Land, where the blessed Sant Yann prepared for the coming of our Saviour, there are people, men and women, marked with the same affliction as herself. For their sake she must return this finger to me *untouched*. Once inside the church you may open the box for the blessing at the altar, but you *must not touch* what is inside or the power of it will be lost. The doctors in Paris, myself among them, need the power preserved, so that one day this disease will not afflict your people, or the people in the Holy Land. They will,' he could not resist a flourish, 'be cleansed as the leper in the River Jordan, whose corrupt flesh became as the flesh of a little child.'

He looked at Le Coadic. 'Does she understand?'

'*Komprenet?*' asked Le Coadic.

'*Ya,*' said the woman, and took the box from Z's reluctant hands.

Around them the murmuring noise of the crowd was swelling into a chant: *an tân! an tân!* They looked up at the church tower, where two or three figures were busy fussing over something at the end of the stretched wire. As the crowd found its voice, a box could be seen trundling its way slowly down the wire towards the huge pile of wood.

Mari-Jobig, between the two men, gave a little grunt of satisfaction. 'The "dragon",' explained Le Coadic, across her. 'It's a mechanism packed with fireworks that – well, you'll see in a minute. They used to have an angel. More poetic, but it was banned, for some reason.'

The box arrived with an audible clunk. There was a popping noise. It was difficult to see quite what happened then, and for a while it seemed as if nothing had. The chant subsided, the people stood subdued; then someone spotted a few thin wisps of smoke, and a pale flowering of flames in the yellow afternoon sun.

Tân! yelled the crowd with relief and surged forward, and then back again as the flames fastened onto the bigger chunks of wood, and fingered and grabbed at the scraps of ribbon and lace, and shrivelled the flowers, and roared.

They had followed Mari-Jobig into the heart of the crowd and found themselves now only a row or two back from the fire. Le Coadic was absorbed in watching a blind man, stood closer than anyone else could bear, his dead eyes turned full into the blaze, his wrinkled face streaming with sweat and tears. Z touched his arm and leaned towards him.

'Shall we go to the church now?' he said 'I'd like to get this over with. I've seen enough from here.'

Le Coadic pulled himself out of his trance and nodded, looking around for Mari-Job. She had vanished in a sea of black dresses and white coiffes.

Up on his balcony, Aubry had started wistfully on his third glass of wine. He was hot, and felt ill, the low pressure affecting him with a dragging lethargy. Although he could not admit it even to himself he was also already aching a little with the loss to come. He picked them out again, near the fire this time, the lanky crumpled figure of Le Coadic in his blueish-grey jacket. Z, indefinably neat and self contained, with a kind of brightness around him. He looked again. They seemed, from their arms, to be arguing. Mari-Jobig was much harder to find in the crowd and he soon stopped trying. What he could see, though, and what everyone on the ground was too busy to notice, were the first rainclouds to reach Brittany in a fortnight, massing up ahead on the coast. Rain, he felt, would be a huge relief.

When he looked back down again the scene had changed. The focus of the crowd had shifted from the roaring fire to a small black-cloaked figure standing on the churchyard wall, with a stick in one hand and something small clasped in the other. He could see Z, and then Le Coadic, pushing their way towards her. All he could do was watch.

They had both spotted her at the same time, clambering awkwardly onto the wall, but it was Z who moved first, cutting through the massed and pushing crowd in a way that left Le Coadic baffled, struggling to keep up. Don't frighten her, he tried to call after him, don't frighten her! The crowd was excited by this departure from the ritual, and everyone strained forward to hear. When Le Coadic finally got close enough he grabbed Z's shoulder and held him firmly.

'What,' hissed Z, all his suavity evaporated by the flames, 'what in the name of all the devils is the woman going to…'

'Don't frighten her,' panted Le Coadic, 'just don't frighten her!'

'I have to get the box before she does something stupid.'

'Listen. She's explaining. About the miracle.'

The familiar rasping voice was fighting the crackle of the fire and the crowd's excitement, but her jubilation was unmistakable.

'*Aotrou Sant Yann.*'

'I've got to get her down.'

'*He let it happen!*'

'In a minute, when she's done.'

'*The knife came down.*'

'She's probably drunk; she'll open the bloody box.'

'*I felt no pain!*'

'She's not drunk.'

'*Aotrou Sant Yann.*'

'She'll open it anyway; I've got to get up there. Help me, man; round the back.'

All the Souls

'See what I bring.'

'Don't let her see you for God's sake.'

'Ar biz torret / heb poan ebet! A finger cut off. With no pain!'

Z had pushed himself to the front of the crowd, as near Mari-Jobig as was possible with the heat from the fire raging at him on one side. He saw Le Coadic climb over the wall further down and start making his way up through the thinner crowd on that side.

She held the box high in her mutilated hand, then lowered it. Z shouted up at her with all his authority.

'Marie-Josèphe! Do not open the box!'

She looked down at him and the frozen face cracked a sideways smile. He moved forward as if to grab at her feet, her skirts, and she prodded him hard in the chest with her staff. The crowd gasped; Z fell back into their arms, spitting his fury.

'Le Coadic!' He yelled. 'Stop her!'

Le Coadic, reaching up behind her, called her name as calmly as he could in all the din, but she scuttled sideways along the wall towards the fire, into the zone too hot to bear. There, silhouetted against the flames, she threw down her stick and brought her free hand to try and open the box.

'Don't open it!' roared Z.

'Mari-Jobig!' called Le Coadic. 'Let me help you!'

Her bent hand scrabbled at the catch. Sweat poured down her lumpy face; her skin flamed red.

Behind the low wall, moving into the unbearable heat, came Le Coadic with his arm outstretched and concern in his eyes. She glanced at him, and carried on fumbling at the box, muttering, determined. At last it flipped open, and with a curious twisting movement she picked up the finger in her stiff hand and waved it triumphantly above her head. Just as Le Coadic reached up to pull her down there was a howl of fury, as Z leapt onto the wall and ran along to grab the finger.

The Collectors

She stepped back from them both, into air, and fell into the fire; as the flames wrapped themselves around her both men saw her impassive face, her startled eyes.

'Poan ebet!' She shouted, astonished. And was gone.

Anaon VIII: Skolan's song

Ma e m'mab Skolan deued aman
Me malloz a leskan gantan!

> If my son Skolan has come here
> I put my curse upon him!

Du e da varh ha du out-te
Peleh oh bet ha da bleh het?

> You in black with the black horse
> where are you going, where have you been?

Deuz ar purgator dond a ran
Ha d'an ivern mond a ran
Gand malloz ma mamm pe meus 'nan

> I have been in purgatory
> I am going to hell
> with my mother's curse upon me

Me meus tremenet nozajo
'tre treid ho kerzeg er parko
Didan ar glao, an erh pe 're
Didan ar skorn pe rielle

> I have spent long nights in the fields
> between the horses' feet
> under the rain and falling snow
> under the ice when it froze

Me lewer bihan 'neus kollet
O hez e e vrasan pehed

> He lost my little book,
> that was his greatest sin.

Purgatory

After an hour or so he sat down to rest on a lump of granite and looked out across the grey sea. Pale light shone intermittently through moving clouds onto one of the small islands ahead; below him the cliffs fell away into waves smashed white by the rocks; gulls dropped and circled. The wind flung handfuls of rain and spray in his face, and he shivered. Perhaps he should just throw the ashes in here and have done.

The rain had arrived ten minutes too late for a miracle, and even then the pelt of fat drops had scarcely ruffled the insatiable fire. No repeat for Mari-Jobig, he thought, of the story of the holy Saint Tecla, miraculously saved from burning by the onset of a storm – now that would have made a ballad. Instead at next year's Sant Yann they will be selling the lamentable and true account of the crazy *kakouzes* who stole the foreign gentleman's watch and leapt into the fire to evade capture. In execrable Breton. He would buy it, of course, for his collection, and only he would know just how lamentable, just how untrue. He stood up and shook himself. He was not properly dressed for rain.

The two doctors had left first thing, Z for Paris with Aubry in tow as far as Saint-Brieuc. Neither had said goodbye. Z had not spoken to him at all since Mari-Jobig fell into the fire, eloquent as he had been with everyone else, taking control of the situation with such grace that to interrupt or make a scene of any kind had been impossible. The victim was, as he had explained to the gendarme in the hotel that evening, a terminally ill patient of his, prone to sudden epileptic attacks – the '*droug Sant Yann*' as you call it do you not? How sadly appropriate. He had recognised the symptoms of an imminent attack and rushed to help her, just too late. Aubry, who had seen the whole thing from his balcony, nodded his confirmation. There was admiration in the gendarme's eyes as Z scribbled a note to Proulx in Morlaix, enclosing a banknote for the victim's elderly mother.

The church authorities had likewise treated the incident with the minimum of fuss. A priest said a prayer over the still hot ashes in the drizzling dawn, and then let everyone back as usual to collect their stones. Le Coadic had hunted in vain for a sign, a trace of her; the little crucifix. A bone. But had settled instead for a handful of ash wrapped in a handkerchief and tucked into the pocket of his coat. He got back to the hotel in time to see Aubry and Z leaving. Over bread and coffee he realised that he could not face Élise and her sadness yet. He packed a knapsack, had the rest of his luggage sent on with a note. Expect me, he wrote, in a day or two.

He threw his apple core over the cliff. The wind caught it, held it up; a gull swooped at it and missed. As he turned to resume his path along the clifftop he felt a rush of air near his head and lifted an arm instinctively, but the bird wheeled off down towards the churning sea and did not attack him again.

Thrift, cushions of the blessed Virgin, made it easy on his feet along the coast. He would try and get round to Loquirec, and down to Plestin. From there, if he had had enough, there would be coaches on the main road to Lannion. Just now, though, he feels he should keep walking for days. It is lucky for him there are so many hours of daylight, even grey, even unreal. He pulls his hat down firmly and continues to make his way around the jagged cliff edge.

The woman in the café at Loquirec was cold. She answered him curtly in French and turned her back on him to clean glasses. He was the only person there, and felt like a stranger, bereft of his charm. He ate his soup with his head bowed, and did not look up to see how little he was reflected in the mottled mirrors. When he had done he left money on the table and bowed courteously towards the counter, but she did not turn round.

Outside the rain had strengthened with the wind; it stung

the left side of his face. He pulled his hat down askew against it and took the road down towards the Corniche; less briskly now, but with his usual walker's lope, he walked for an hour or more in the sideways push of the wind round another headland to St Efflam. Here he bought bread and sausage and strawberries, and ate them in the churchyard, out of sight of the road. Water dripped and drizzled off the eaves and the guttering; blessing, he supposed, the small souls of surreptitiously buried babies, dead before the baptism that would have seen them straight to heaven. Were they properly looked after over there, he wondered, not for the first time, were there nurses? Mothers dead in childbirth and aching-full of ghostly milk? That would be beautiful and very moving, he thought. She might like that. He hoped she might like that. He would have to have a chapter on the souls of children, of course, whatever happened.

Ahead of him stretched the Lieue de Grève, a huge half-moon of flat sand disappearing into the mist, and the grey sea beyond. It was low tide, the sand would be firm to walk on, and he could save a few kilometres by crossing in a straight line to St Michel. By then, he thought, he would perhaps have had enough, he would be able to rest, find a coach to take him to a decent hotel in Lannion. He felt better, lighter, He thought the wind had dropped a little.

The rain had emptied the Lieue de Grève of the usual June crowds of English and Parisians come to paddle and play. A few scattered figures could be seen near the top of the beach, walking or busy with nets; others had baskets for cockling. Mist blurred the far end of the bay but Le Coadic was on familiar territory by now; days out as a child, collecting shells; now he sometimes came looking for stories and songs from the cockle-pickers and fishermen and women mending nets. He might, he thought, meet one of his favourite informants out there. He felt that he would not mind a little company now.

He cut down from the road, through bracken and over the little rocks and pebbles and the crunch of the gravel to the firm-packed silky sand, patterned with wavy ridges and the sheen of water. The sea itself was a long way out, dissolved in mist; he picked out the spire at St Michel and set off towards it. The clouds were definitely brightening. His stick made a line of vanishing dints in the wet sand to his right; had he looked behind him he might have noticed that his boots left barely a trace.

Iou, Iou. The gull cry was strangled, weird, somewhere ahead.

Iannik an Aod, said a voice inside his head. The voice was Fañch Riou, he decided, a lobster and crab fisher from up near Plougrescant: played the fiddle, sang very badly. Hush, Fañch, he thought, not now.

Iannik eo, ah ya, said the voice again urgently. *Klevet peus?*

Gouelan, retorted Le Coadic briskly. It's a gull. *Meus klevet, ya.* I heard it. He kept walking.

Iou, Iou.

To his left, he thought, this time, although seagulls were not good indications of direction at the best of times. Iannik, drowned and angry, would at least emerge, he supposed, from the sea.

Fañch had never actually seen him, of course, only heard him a few times when he was down on the beach hauling up nets after dark in bad weather. His grandfather had, though, or so said his grandmother, a few days before he went to the bottom of the sea and two weeks before he washed up as a tattered grey body on the shoreline at Plougrescant. Holy Virgin be blessed, his gran had said, relieved to have a body to bury.

Poor Iannik, thought Le Coadic. But not now. Not yet. Leave me be.

And then there was water sloshing around his ankles and a darkish shape in the whiteness of the fog ahead of him like a person. But the crying was definitely that of a gull. He was walking straight into the sea. Something white swooped at him; he put his arms up to protect his eyes and heard a man's voice, a voice he knew, shouting horribly for help. He turned full about and ran stumbling into the fog.

His fingers had blood on them and he picked at the wet knots of his boots, tipping seawater out onto the bracken beside him. He felt again, more gently this time, for the cut on his face. He had fallen over rocks coming off the beach, cutting his hand and scraping his cheekbone. He felt for the handkerchief in his breast pocket, remembered the ash, and wiped his hands clean on the wet cushion of thrift instead. Damp moss cleaned his face, and he stood up to get his bearings. The thick fog hung a hundred yards away, but here at the land's edge it was clearer, a thinnish mist dissipating with a new breeze. It still took him a long moment to understand where he was, his mind struggling to recognise the ghost of a spire rising further down the coast to his left. If that was St Michel he was much further up the coast than he expected, and he still felt baffled at how sea and fog had conspired to rub out his infallible sense of place. But he had the sun now, weak and oddly lacking in warmth, and the faint curve of the bay and the spire: he would go inland, pick up one of the small cart roads to take him back to the Lannion road. He would not refuse a lift, if one came his way. He had done his penance. He would find a decent hotel.

Encouraged, putting aside his recent shock, he pushed his way slowly through a coastal belt of gorse and bracken and brambles, all dripping wet and laced with shivering webs that he left torn and hanging in his wake. At last he reached the banked-up stone hedge, the *kleuz*, the talus, of a field and pulled himself onto it, snagging in hawthorn and gorse. The mist was almost gone here, but the fine drizzle blanked everything beyond the middle distance. No houses that he could see, but now that he was in farmed land the network of hedges and tracks would pull him in towards buildings and the main road. As he clambered awkwardly down the other side a small branch of hawthorn snapped off in his hand, releasing a scatter of water drops and a handful of souls. He thought again of the woman's ashes in his pocket and, having located the gate at the far end of the field, set himself to thinking what best to do with them.

What a shame, he thought again, that the fire had not left even a tiny chip of bone. He rummaged in his memory for the details; the squint-eyed seamstress from Plougasnou who had explained with some satisfaction how to unmask a murderer by wrapping the victim's smallest fingerbone in your handkerchief and then 'Excuse me,' you say, 'I think you may have lost this' and clenching it in your fist like an amiable grandparent playing hiding games with a little child you pass the bundle unseen right into your suspect's hands and – if you have the right person of course – wait for the cry of pain, the curse, the astonished guilty face gazing at the red welt blistering across the palm. His olive-skinned musician's hands, branded. Oh, he killed her, the devil, I was only trying to save her. A small packet of ash through the post, perhaps, unwrapped over breakfast. But at the best it would give him a rash, he supposed, and scorch his linen tablecloth; it would not mark him as he deserved.

He was in a sunken lane which must lead to the farm. The trees had grown up high on either side, forming a tunnel. Big-boned beeches curved in to meet above his head, their green, usually too intense, muted by the drizzle which they were holding off him. Where was everyone? Tregor at midsummer, where were they all? No sign of cattle in any field, and the hoofprints in the still solid mud did not look fresh; it was too quiet, the birds were not loud enough and all he could hear were rustling noises overhead as a breeze he could not feel made the leaves whisper. Once there was an old woman, and an old man, and they died and became beech trees, and because she had not given enough to the poor in her lifetime she was cold, cold; but because he had, now and again, and because he made sure their children did too he had a dispensation for them both to go and warm up by the fire at their son's house, now and again; and there was nothing more pathetic and more frightening than the sound of those two huge trees shuffling and rustling towards the warmth. He was cold now, and this beech tunnel seemed to have no end. It grew darker as the rustling trees blocked out the grey light and the fine drizzle. Every minute he expected to see signs of settlement, an opening out; he expected, at least, to hear the sounds of daily life, but it was all his own breathing and the faint hiss of leaves and the curiously distant birdsong. And the further he walked the more it seemed that this track, of all the paths in Brittany, was the only one to resist the hardening drought, that the further he went, the muddier it got. Soon there were puddles in the cart ruts and runnels of brown water along the edges, and late celandine and moss in a vivid poisonous green, and the going was increasingly difficult for him. The lane appeared to be without end. With the sun hidden his sense of direction began to fail him again, and he could feel a new edge of anxiety nudging at his mind, telling him that again, in the heart of his childhood country, he was out of place, *dépaysé*. All he could do was push on, knowing that there was no cart track in the whole of Brittany that did not have some sense to it, and that this one would come to its senses in the end.

Le Coadic thought less about the old woman now and more about Élise. He would go straight to Port Blanc from Lannion; that evening if he could, but certainly tomorrow morning, and by the quickest means he could find. They would eat a long meal together and then if she were well enough they could walk down to the harbour and he would tell her the story somehow, though that would depend on her. He had been away collecting nearly five weeks and she would know by now if this pregnancy had made it beyond the fourth month. After so many losses he was resigned to one more. His sisters would be there, he thought, if it had happened again. Perhaps his brother-in-law would come too, that would be some comfort, to talk to a friend. He was glad of their affection, their concern, but afraid that the women would keep her from him, fussing, protective.

The salt-water in his socks had given him a blister and the longer he walked in the muddy tracks the more the pain of it pushed away all other thoughts. The rough wool rubbing on the patch of raw skin forced him to change his stride; soon he was limping. The hole felt deeper, redder, more gouged out with every step, and he thought of the bloodied women in the ballads shuffling penitentially, absurdly, on their knees thrice round the church, or all the way to Rome or Compostela to die a good death absolved by their scraped-away flesh. But he had had enough of his guilt by now. It did not brace him.

At last the pain halted him and he sat down at the edge of the track and impatiently unknotted the muddy boot again, peeling off the thick wet wool. He packed green moss around the sore and forced his foot back in. As he was tying up the laces he heard a noise ahead, a creaking grincing noise; a cart. He hurried up towards it and found that at last the tunnel had opened onto a broader crossroads; approaching from his left, slowly, was a large cart loaded with sacks, pulled by a small dirty horse.

'*Mad an traoù?*' He lifted a hand in greeting and smiled at the carter with huge relief. The cart stopped a few paces beyond Le Coadic and a yellowish face looked back over a shoulder and motioned him to climb in among the sacks.

'*Da Lannuon?*' said Le Coadic, though he did not much care where he ended up.

'*Ya.*' The man clicked his tongue and the short horse set off again, very slowly, jolting and creaking into a now tangible drizzle. Le Coadic twice tried to talk to him, to find out the name of the nearest farm, but the man would say nothing further. It was like being in a foreign country, he thought again, baffled, but he made himself as comfortable as he could among the knobbly hessian sacks, pulled his hat down over his face, and slept.

Anaon IX: Pool

When the pale carter tipped him out like a sack of potatoes, with a sack of potatoes, at the top of the lane, the thrill around the pool was palpable. *He's coming, he's coming*; it passed like a shudder through the anaon, pressed closer together than silver sardines; *the book man, the man who knows the rules, he's coming to us at last.*

Those who saw him stagger down the muddy lane in the gathering dark, with a split sackful of potatoes rolling like little skulls after him, will testify to his anger, his confusion and his growing fear. It is steep down to our pool, and although he wanted to turn back and run after the cart and its slow horse the forward momentum kept him stumbling downward till it was too late to stop and who knows, he may have seen the silver flickering of our understandable excitement and thought it meant a house or somesuch, and so he carried on.

Down to where the alders start to close in, and how heartily sick he is now of the traditional sunken lane with its branches clasped in prayer blocking out the sky. Down to where no habitation could ever be because even the trees here are ankle deep in water that glimmers when it gets any light to glimmer by. Down, then, to the edge of the dark pool, where willow and alder crowd and tangle thousands of branches hung with millions of souls. And not just souls, because here is one of those places that certain groups of people recognise for what it is, and they have, for a long while now, been leaving us scraps of cloth and small coins, but very secretly, so it is not in any of his books. Not yet, at any rate.

What does he do? He stands, afraid and astonished. He puts a hand out to touch the white strips of cotton tied to the twigs of the nearest branch. The moon finally pushes its way out of the drizzle and gives him enough light to grasp the size of the pool, and the sheer number of cotton strips hanging damp and rather lifeless on either side. In spite of himself, his fear, his fatigue, he wonders which saint owns this place. We try to tell him, none, but it seems that he canot hear us. He squats down at the muddy edge of the pool and looks about for a stone well, a spring, a votive centre. He won't find one, it doesn't work like that here. He sits there for a long time in the damp, looking blank.

Some of the anaon are restless as hell. They were probably expecting a speech or something, a grand gesture. An explanation. Instead, he sits there, an exhausted man with an exhausted mind, too tired to rise to the occasion of his life. After a bit he pulls back from the edge of the pool and more or less collapses into the bracken at the edge of the path, leaving us, less than contented, to whisper and fuss.

The weather saves us all. He lies for about an hour, crushed and beyond the reach of moonlight or fine drizzle or thorns, but then a proper heavy Breton rain sets in and forces him back on his poor feet. This time he has more sense, seems more himself, or at any rate himself as we know him through the gossips, at second, third, fourth, ten-thousandth hand. He stands properly upright and faces the pool, which is dancing with thick black drops. He reaches into his jacket, soaked and filthy and torn, and finds the folded handkerchief. He opens it out and cradles it in one hand, dips a finger in the ash and marks his forehead. Then he flicks the cloth so that the ash scatters across the water. It hisses, of course, as it falls. There is a ripping sound as he tears the handkerchief with his teeth and ties the strips round the alder twigs on either side of where he stands. Then he says, very calmly, that he is sorry for what happened to the woman, and he turns and walks away, stumbling along a muddy track he can barely see, knowing that if he keeps going long enough the morning will return and show him the way, and that if he cannot keep going the morning will come anyway. The anaon, it must be said, are terribly impressed.

Return

No one knows how long he walked for this time. But he woke on his back looking into a blue sky through the protective fronds of green bracken. They towered above him, smelling of childhood and home, and he lay for a while trying to remember where he was, and why. But that was quite beyond him. He sat up then, and looked at the scratches and bruises on his arms and hands and his knees where the cloth of his trousers had ripped away, and at the thick stems of the bracken like a small forest around him. Some of the fronds were still uncurling, little bunched-up fists, like a baby's hand tight round an adult finger, like green soldiers ready to fight.

Itron Varia da Borz Wenn
A ra soudarded deus radenn

> Notre Dame de Port Blanc
> Made soldiers out of ferns

That was all he knew of the song, all that anyone knew perhaps, though he'd asked for it long and hard around his native village. She was supposed to have saved us by turning every single stem of bracken into a soldier and terrifying the living daylights out of the bloody English, massed in their ships and ready to pounce out beyond the Sept Îles. What an army that must have been. Hundreds of them gathered around him now, though they seemed to have come in peace this time. He tried getting to his feet. Even then the bracken reached his waist. He looked for the track he should have made last night, as a partial memory came back to him of crashing and tearing for hours through the leaves and the brambles before falling over once too often and failing to get back up. It was very strange, he thought, that there should be no trace at all of how he got there. Nothing broken. Nothing flattened. Nothing torn.

But he could feel the sea not far away now, and knew what

he had to do: head for the higher ground, where granite boulders pushed above the army of fronds like fortresses. Something in the colour of the rock made his heart leap, but he kept his mind very deliberately, very methodically, on the task of getting the tight mass of soldiers to yield a path. He had lost his hazel walking stick somewhere on this stupid journey, and there was nothing in sight with which to replace it. *Itron Varia da Borz Gwenn / A ra soudarded deus radenn.* Come on, *paotred*, he said, let me through, I'm on your side.

Climbing the steps up from the beach he knew he was a strange sight. They were used to seeing him arrive at odd times, weary and little dusty perhaps from the roads, but not like this, tramp-ragged, worn out, cut, bruised and in pain. In his left hand, instead of the straight hazel, he still clutched, unthinking, a twisted bit of oak torn off a fallen tree he'd clambered over, half-buried under the bracken, and used to beat a way through. It would sit on his desk for years, and help him write. He could see a face, he said, in one of the knots; he called it Skolan, as a private joke. It was not, he came to realise, a comforting or a happy face, but by the time he came to write the angry postscript to the Book there was, in any case, precious little comfort or happiness to be had. His boy would spend his childhood afraid of it, but would take it for luck, bad luck as it turned out, into the Great War.

He kept his hat pulled down, as if afraid to be recognised, but it was more from fatigue than anything because he knew that any recognition now, after so long amongst strangers, would only make him glad. God, he hoped that she would be there, at home, on her own, and he took the little steps quickly in spite of the pain in his feet, passing the workers in the lower cottages with barely a nod. Up past the sail-menders, past the crab and lobster pots, and now he could see the house on the rise, foursquare, elegant, framed by the curving dark pine. And he was just passing the tiny dark cottage of the seamstress, Lise Bellec, when he heard her thin voice float out above the sound of his own laboured breath. *Itron Varia*, she sang,

Itron Varia da Borz Gwenn
A ra soudarded deus radenn

She did indeed, he thought, and then, that's not the right tune. He slowed in spite of himself and held his breath as another couplet floated out. A new one. He stopped altogether. And another.

She knows it! Twenty years I've been asking and she knows it!

He hesitated then. He wanted to knock and stoop and enter where he had been so many times before and claim this prize, this reward for his endurance at his journey's end. But then it wasn't quite his journey's end and he was hoping, had been hoping all along, for a different reward, and he was superstitious enough, soap and clean linen notwithstanding, to feel that two rewards, two endings, would really be pushing his luck, and that, as far he knew, he really had no more luck left to push. So he carries on, with the new tune already in his head, up through the village to the old schoolmaster's house, their house, where, this time, he will find her alone and contented, just coming in from the garden with a basket full of peas.

Postscript

Here is your book, people, anaon, here is your natural history of the dead. Anecdotes collected, categorised, gathered into groups: the themes run through them like connecting veins, their images are cold flesh. I have written it in French to give it more authority, the clarity of distance, and to allow for international comparison of types. You will be world famous, people, anaon, though you will also be doomed, like my father, my sisters and my brother-in-law whom you left to die when their little boat capsized off the coast of Plougrescant. No folk braver than your fishermen on the whole north coast; no folk more deeply in thrall to the idiotic tyrannies of the dead. You heard him cry; all night you heard him, the survivor. He was a fine scholar, a bright mind, a husband, my brother and my friend. He was close enough to see lights in your cottage windows. He could not understand why you did not come. I do. You thought he was a soul in purgatory, and you were frightened.

You may, as he did, take a little while to die. But these words, anaon, are the nails in your coffin. These white pages are your winding sheets.

Camera Obscura

We're sitting in the sun like a couple of lizards on a ledge halfway up the north face of the Avon Gorge. There is an old metal railing between us and the drop and I have never felt so comfortable in all my life. Below us the A4 runs its swift and glittering course; the Avon, leached by the tide, is mostly dissipated into mud. The bridge, the marvellous bridge, does what it does best: looks grand, spanning the gorge to our left, ignoring the river's poor show. Did I say I was comfortable? I am more than comfortable, I am practically purring.

You would not think, I tell him as he strokes a little pattern on my left hand, you wouldn't think, would you, that I've just seen a ghost?

No, he says, holding my weak wrist experimentally between a large thumb and forefinger and then moving round for a pulse. You don't feel like someone who's just seen a ghost. Where did you see it?

Him, I say. Not it. In there. When we were in there.

Behind us a tunnel and steps cut into the rock lead back up into the building housing the Camera Obscura. Clifton spreads out green and elegant around it. Inside, in small groups, people stand peering over the rail into a white paper pool, waiting for the blurry images to settle.

It *was* a bit like a seance, he says. How did you know? That he was a ghost?

Have you ever been to a seance? I ask. I am genuinely interested, in spite of the slow fingers in the crook of my arm.

No.

Me neither.

The sandstone loves the sun as much as I do, and though it is only March it is warming up nicely. I lean back into it and close my eyes.

Clifton, elegant Clifton, with its green park and fine houses, lurches around in the pool below us. We watch it upside down, holding hands in the dark. They are trying to find the bridge. At last they leave and I get my chance to control the lever, the joystick that swivels the eye of the lens. I am methodical, practised from all those hours at home, and although it is his town, and he names the places as they swim into view, I am better than him at getting a slow sweep, at capturing and holding scenes. The surprise, however often you do it, is always the same. You settle on a picture, get it still, just right, and then something moves across it. A dog, a car, a gull, a breaking wave. The images are small, grainy and dulled and it is a mystery to me why this should be so much more astonishing than watching a film, or doing a conference by videolink, or spying on the neighbours with Google Streetmap. But it is. And the moving things always look oddly vulnerable.

The fingers consider the gap between the sleeve of my dress and my upper arm. I check to see if the bridge is still standing and close my eyes again.

I recognised him; I've seen him before.

He makes the mildly interested noise of someone too preoccupied, or too lazy, to speak.

In Aber, I say, in the Camera Obscura there.

The fingers take off like birds and when I open my eyes there he is, sitting forward, hugging his knees, looking at me sideways.

Camera Obscura

What? he says. What are you talking about?

So I do exactly the same, hug my knees and look at him sideways.

I've seen him before, I explain very slowly, as to an idiot. In the Camera Obscura at the top of Constitution Hill in Aberystwyth.

He thinks about that for a second and then grins, and he is so lovely when he grins that I have to laugh, and we both laugh, and I move up for him to put his arm round me and soon enough the fingers are examining the gap in the other sleeve, and I leave it at that.

But I was telling the truth, of course. I have seen him before, and often enough, to know him, even blurred, even walking away. The shock this time was to find him here; if my pulse had been taken twenty minutes earlier, before the sun and the honeyed sandstone contrived to slow everything down, I know it would have been quick. I was even, briefly, faintly scared: he was much closer, for one thing, if no clearer as a result, somewhere on the green parkland around the sweeping lens. Not knowing the place that well I couldn't tell which side, or how close, but it looked as if he was walking with long strides up a slope. The children fighting over the joystick were intent on capturing the bridge, and didn't hold him. By the time I got my chance to look for him, he'd gone.

At home he is often on the beach, or walking along the prom just above it. Sometimes he leans on the railings and looks out to sea, and once I caught him skimming stones. He has also been known to wander in the maze of bracken paths above the golf-course, and once, tantalisingly, he appeared to be passing the weather station just behind the Camera building. But on the whole he prefers the seafront. The range of the lens suits him, I expect, though it maddened me: too far to see properly, but close enough to recognise. He always wears the same clothes, dark with a red scarf , even when it's warm. A couple of times he has been closer, but then he blurs so badly that even if he did turn his face towards me it wouldn't help.

To start with I assumed he was real. I had discovered that the ramshackle cafe at the top of the hill was a safer place than the library to read or work without interruptions, and had taken to going up perhaps a couple of mornings a week, leaving my phone at home. Apart from the bouncy castle, for which I consider myself too old, the Camera Obscura was the only real displacement activity bar brisk walks around the top, of which I did plenty, and I soon found it a compelling and surprisingly relaxing way of avoiding difficult footnotes. The second or third time I saw him in the big white disc I got curious, and started half-expecting to pass him in town. The time after that he was on the beach and I went straight out onto the viewing balcony, only to find that it was a crucial few feet lower than the lens, and had no view at all of the closest stretch of prom. Several days later I located him sitting on the top bench nearest the kicking bar, and ran out past the cafe to the edge of the hill where you get a decent view down. I was a little surprised not to see him then. He must be right at the top of the beach hidden by the cliff, I thought, or, and this made my heart skip a little, he could have started climbing up here. I walked down the zig-zag path to the bottom, psyched-up for an encounter with a man I was more than curious to meet, and met no one. He can't, I thought, have taken the cliff-train up. Can he? Even at that distance, he didn't look the type. But just to be sure I half-ran, half-walked all the way up to the top again and peered into the cafe, and the gift shop, and the Camera itself. No one. At which point common sense shamed me into going home and doing some washing.

I left the place alone for several days after that and worked hard in the library, finishing a chapter for my supervisor more or less when I'd promised it, to her evident surprise. The final chapter, however, was almost entirely written in the red and white cafe at the top of Constitution Hill, and the writing of it ran concurrently with a careful campaign of verification (or, as it turned out, rather the reverse) involving random spot checks from the Camera and a certain amount of nifty legwork up and down the hill. I ate a lot of flapjack, but became extremely fit. In the end, having almost convinced myself, I did what I should have done nearer the beginning and arranged to meet a friend in the cafe before casually suggesting a quick peek at Pen Dinas and the rooftops of Aber. There he was, obligingly, leaning on the railings looking out to sea. When my friend couldn't see anything except a large woman leading three white dogs, I accepted the truth, and, with a twist of regret, revised my romantic expectations accordingly. Then came that brilliant conference in Birmingham where I met Paul, and then three months of frantic rewriting and checking to get the thesis done by December as I had promised them in the interview. And then the days out, like this one, exploring Bristol, looking for a flat for us to move into.

I don't mind him being here, though I am surprised. I thought that ghosts needed places, and assumed that his place was Aber. Him being here suggests, as I had begun to suspect, that he needs me more than he needs the place. I don't mind that, I find it rather gratifying. Or, and this has only just occurred to me, it may mean that his place is the Camera, but that I have to be there to make him happen. I start to wonder, in my sun-induced trance, if I will feel obliged to construct a glittering academic career entirely around posts in university towns rejoicing in – whatever is the plural? Camerae obscurae; camerata obscuranta; cameras obscuras… I don't do languages. And then I have an idea that blows over me like light spray from a fountain. It wakes me up. We'll do a Grand Tour, in Paul's decrepit yellow Ford Fiesta, of all the places in Britain that have them. Slowly, slowly, I reach up and unclasp the warm fingers from the nape of my neck. Then I stand up and grab his shoulder as the gorge gapes dizzily below me. The blue eyes open, and look up. Come on, I say. Come on. I've got some research to do.

Absolution

It must have slipped in while I was taking the bags out to the car on Friday.

I imagine it blowing round the house, in and out of rooms, whipping the curtains, pushing itself up against the window panes. I imagine it testing the blocked-up chimney, being baffled by the woodburner; I see it vortexing up and down the stairs, increasingly anxious, increasing in velocity, until finally, in the back kitchen, it burst open the double doors of the French window and escaped, buffeting the little flowering cherry before twisting, flipping back on itself like a huge invisible salmon to take off up the hill and away.

As soon as I got the front door open on Sunday night I knew that the cold air was different in kind from the retracted cold of the house left alone for the weekend. I walked through to the back, cautiously turning on lights with an outstretched hand, to find the doors wide open to the wet night and a scattering of black leaves on the tiles. I left the leaves and pulled the doors to, locking them this time. I did a quick, brave, scout for burglars in all the other rooms in the house, and then put the heating on for an hour, because it was cold and I wanted to hear the boiler's chunder. I made tea and toast and put the radio on. After a while I unpacked my stuff and went to bed.

All the Souls

Rain woke me early. I padded peacefully around the house in my pyjamas, reclaiming it, inspecting the rooms for traces of the wind's incursion. There were none. That picture had probably been skewed for a while; there were the usual piles of paper on the desk, nothing underneath. The dark chocolate petals of the tulips on the windowsill had fallen gently around the vase. Nothing even to hint at that prowling, nervous presence I imagined turning anxious circles in the sanctuary of my clean, bright house. Of course, being reasonable, and with some respect for the laws of physics, I knew that the gust would have been instantaneous, straight in and out. But I kept half-looking for signs as I headed back upstairs to get ready for work. The swirl of coloured clothes on the floor in the girls' room was not new either. I picked up a few socks automatically, and stood there, missing their morning fuss and bother, planning treats for their return. Then I woke myself up properly with a shower, got dressed and drove off to the office. I wondered if he would have sent me an email.

He hadn't. I worked stultifyingly late, hoarding hours to make time for the girls when they came back from their father's later in the holidays. The migraine came on as I drove home, eating away at the edges of my vision, turning the windscreen into an abstract splatter of drizzle and light; the car had to find its own way for the last mile up the hill through the dark lanes. I swallowed painkillers, more tea, and went to bed early, sleeping deeply under a mountain of stratified quilts and blankets. I find it so hard to keep warm.

What happened then? What happened? I was suddenly awake. An animal leapt across me from out of the bed. Grey-brown, shorthaired, larger than a rabbit, smaller than a deer. Neither cat nor dog. Did I cry out? In seconds I was out on the landing in the shocking cold air of two in the morning; then I was in Alice's little bed, curled over in fear, desperate for a child to hold. I groped around until I found one of her rag dolls and pushed it hard into the space under my rib cage where the shock felt worst. It took several minutes, I think, before I started to breathe again properly. For a long while I lay in the tiny bed and suffered the lurching sensation of trying to hold two wholly incompatible states together. Like the other Alice, I thought briefly, and with sudden compassion; grown so big so fast, poor thing. But was she this frightened? I don't remember. I gradually quieted my breathing so that I could hear if the creature downstairs was trying to get out, but the rain was hammering on the sky-light and pouring off the eaves, and I could hear nothing except the sound of its ferocious cleansing. It must be running off in streams, I thought. And then there was no way of avoiding the thought of them all, pathetic little scraps, buried for surreptitious baptism under the slate skirts of church roofs; *nameless me*, they cry, according to tradition, to bloody superstition, *nameless me*.

It had been an exceptional day. As good a reason as any, we agreed, to make it the last. At first I had been tense and resentful. The food in the posh pub was nothing special, and we did not seem to have much to say. But afterwards we walked by the river, and, after a month of rain, the late February sun came out cold and bright on fierce brown water grown to twice its normal size. It was almost at the top of the old bridge, pushing against the stone and through the drowned arches, too fast, I thought, and too powerful. But we were hypnotised; I relented, relaxed. He took my cold hand. Come on, he said, I'll show you a secret.

We climbed over a stile onto a footpath that led away from the river, all elder and brambles and mud. After about half a mile we came across a building with a copse of ash trees to one side. There was a raucous rookery in the trees; the birds, the clumps of nest and the thin branches were all sharp and dark against the washed-out blue sky. Naturally I wasn't surprised when the building turned out to be a little church, tucked into a damp mossy graveyard littered with snowdrops, celandines and early primroses. Most of our days out involved a visit to a church. Neither of us has much time for Christianity, and I actively disapprove of God, but after what happened I suspect we were both inclined to some sort of penance; and we both love churches, at least the right sort. This small plain building with criss-crossed glass windows looked like the right sort.

He held back, deliberately of course, taking pictures of gravestones. I felt that I already knew what this place would be like: simple, with polished oak pews, Sunday's flowers, a plaque or two for the war dead and the local squire on the whitewashed walls. Perhaps it was a decorated font he wanted me to see; a leaping hare or a little grinning creature carved into the misericord. There was always something. I pushed at the thick door several times before it gave. When I did get it open it took a long moment to understand what I could see.

The thick curve of stone pillars; the uneven floor and walls, paint flaking off them in the warm burnt reds and yellows of an Italian fresco. I moved forward as though into a wood, unable to grasp its shape: everything curved inwards. A Virgin and Child carved on a wall were so worn away that they too were just curves, protective curves round a blank little head. I could not look at her, and turned my face upwards to the windows. The cold, clean squares of the criss-crossed glass made the pale, bright world outside look fluid: underwater rooks, the snagging twigs like weeds, like a lost alternative version of the ones I had just passed. I think it was the loss, the loss of the alternative, that hurt. It felt as if all of time had been compressed in there. It took the breath from me. By the time he came in I was helpless, crying.

We sat outside on a grave slab, snowdrops at our feet, and he put his arm around me. I buried my head in his winter coat and found after a bit that I could breathe again. Words came back to us one by one, until there were enough to make a bridge, a thin and rickety bridge at first, but firming up quickly, first to consciousness, and then to affection, and then – safest of all, dry land – to wit. When the wind bit too sharply we headed back for the car in search of tea and cake, and found the perfect place, all doilies and black-and-white waitresses. The rest of the afternoon we were our funny, ironic selves, and even our last goodbyes at the station were so *Brief Encounter* we could only laugh.

The girls came home. School started again and the days got warmer and busier. The creature, like the wind, must have found a way out; it didn't come back, or at least I don't think it did. For several weeks, with the headaches, I had this sense of something colourless and formless moving just beyond my line of vision. I stopped trying to catch it, and eventually I was bothered by nothing more than a ripple and a shadow, rather like the effect of looking through old glass. I always lock the back doors now, but have taken to leaving the kitchen window open just a crack, in case.

It was a good while later that he sent the map, marked with a scattering of little black circles. The scrawl on the attached yellow Post-it said, *I'll be in the visitors' books; look me up.* And I thought, you know, I might do that, over the months, the years, if ever I happen to find myself in the right place.

Warrior

At last it was cleared. Then he could work alone, with the borrowed horse, at churning up the ground, breaking and tearing the remaining roots. The slowness could have been painful, but he was a persistent man, and besides, each line of turned earth gave him the deepest pleasure.

They had been good. His brother, a neighbour and his son, all of them at it with scythes and picks and their scratched dirty hands hacking at bramble and bracken and lugging the bigger stones to the edges to shore up the existing collapsed wall and delimit the reclaimed field. On and off it had taken a whole week, and now it was good to be on his own up there, getting below the surface of his field. Sometimes he stopped and looked out across to the sea or down the slope to the cottage. The wind, they all said, would be ruinous, it would blight. In that hot week he could only wonder about the wind, but he figured nonetheless how he would take it on. He pondered strategies as he and the horse went slowly up and slowly down, and even this gave him pleasure.

Of all of them, flushed and beginning to ache in the dirty carriage, he felt the most injured, the most cheated, and he counted his losses in a silent, introverted rage. Anaig and the baby he passed over quickly, he could not even think about them yet. There was the unpaid debt of his neighbour's harvest; it hurt him not to repay the loan of that patient horse, the hours of work on the hill. There was the waste of the work itself, the undoing of their shared labour. He felt the brambles and the bracken massing, gathering strength. They would take back the land, he thought, his own providential bit of land.

The flowers thrown around the carriage were wilting as they pulled up at a station to stretch their legs and be served coffee by the women of the Red Cross. They milled around dazed, grateful for the comparative cool. Children stood on railings to watch them. More flowers were thrown. Girls pouring coffee felt licensed to stare into their eyes, and did so. They piled back into the carriages with renewed faith in themselves and began singing. He didn't join in.

As night came on most of them spread grey cloaks and made shift to sleep on their lumpy haversacks. He sat wedged upright in a corner, and continued to think about his field and his loss. It was more than just the field, or the beauty of owning it: three days ago he had found something, and now he was halfway to the Front and had not even had the time to understand what it was. The plough had snagged, up towards the rise of the bank. He'd unhitched the horse, thinking to give up for the day, and gone back to see what was wrong. There were a couple of flattish stones, not big: he threw them over the bank. But it hadn't been the stones; there was something else caught in the blades. He pulled it out of the soil and brushed it clumsily.

It was smaller than his hand, greenish metal under the dirt. The curving lowered neck and small head of a bird, and then wings with stylised feathers pulled back to form a crest. A swan. He held it more carefully and felt his heart beat: it had a lovely shape. He stroked some of the dirt off it and turned it over and over, liking the curve of the neck. He couldn't think what it was.

Putting it down gently beside him he bent back to the ground. The plough was still in the way, so he dragged it forward himself. On hands and knees then he had scraped and found clay, in a neatly circular patch paler than the rest of the soil. It was hard for his fingers to dig out, but he did not have to get far to find more greenish metal, and feel something spherical. By now it was almost dark, so he piled earth back on top and marked the place with a stem of bracken. He took the horse by the bridle and led it home down the hill.

All that night between the packs, between dark bouts of sleep, his hand searched out the swan in his pocket and his big square index finger stroked the curving neck.

The following morning he had worked for Yann. They were just starting to cut in the lower field, and he was deep in the thought of his discovery. He did not register the news, now certain, of their imminent departure; it did not touch him. But returning home at midday he found Anaig quietly and angrily making the necessary arrangements. For the first time in their lives together they had eaten in silence, and the shock of it caught up with him at last. While she fed the baby he had clumsily and unexpectedly made coffee, which made her laugh, and in the relieved air they were able to discuss the details of his leaving. He was careful in his phrasing to get her to tell him what he should have known already but had ignored.

They had teased him when he asked Yann for a final afternoon's loan of the peaceable horse, but he had to finish his field. The bracken stem hung exhausted in the heat. He did not go over to it, but began ploughing from the far end, shifting the last stones and leading the horse for two mindless hours until finally the clean soils met and it was done, all except the small patch up near the bank. He muttered some words of thanks and set the horse free to graze.

The topsoil came away easily with his hands, and then it was solid. He had brought a knife and a trowel, and with these he dug away at the packed clay, following the contours of the metal. It was soon very clearly a head, wearing a helmet, blurred with clay and dirt, and he saw that he wanted water to wash it clean. Thinking of water brought on a terrible thirst. He had worked in the heat all afternoon and was dizzy with it. Retrieving a leather bottle from his jacket by the wall, he crouched over the shallow pit, the head emerging strangely at its centre, and very carefully poured water, a little at a time, onto the parts where the clay stuck most, helping it off with his fingers. His thumbs pushed suddenly through empty eye sockets. The last drops of water smoothed dirt from the curve of a neck. The thirst burned in his throat.

It was streaked with persistent earth, but good enough. Clear in its expression, and serious, perhaps sad. A young face, he thought, a youth or a young woman, it was hard to tell, though he had seen that clear and serious look on Anaig. A warrior's helmet. He went back to his jacket for the swan-crest and fitted it into its place, then stood back and looked, a little afraid, at this strange figure in his field, buried up to the neck and staring sadly ahead with empty eyes. And then he looked up at the day and knew that was enough. He took the horse down to Yann for the last time, refused a drink, and went home.

All night, under the massed light of tiny stars, the freed head in the field stared in the direction of the black sea. At dawn the man rose and climbed up to the place once more. He filled in the pit with newly ploughed earth and dragged a flat stone over it. The swan went back in his pocket.

He heard horses scream. He learned to curse fluently in French. His body was taught how to march while hung about absurdly with pots and pans, tent canvas, spade, spare shoes, more canvas, square dry biscuits, dried soup, coffee bags, salt and sugar. He became the member of the division allotted to carry the coffee grinder: he learned to make excellent coffee. He learned to play cards. He saw blood on the German soldiers a stone's throw from their line. For some reason they were always near the Front. *Plenty more where you come from,* said a senior officer to them. *Y'en aura toujours, des Bretons.*

The brother who had helped clear the field was killed after two months. He went home three times in three years. Anaig was back with her parents, and their little house on the hillside was empty; his child changed impossibly from one visit to the next. As the war dug itself into the ground he came to depend utterly on the changing sky to relieve the pressure of the tonnes and tonnes of earth in which they had sunk.

The ten or so years after the war were increasingly unhappy, because of the headaches and a creeping fatigue, like ivy, which slowly took away his strength. It was difficult for him to acknowledge this invisible damage, and he worked himself much harder than his body could bear, coming home afterwards to be silent all evening. When the children were asleep, he put his head down on the table and wept. At last he hurt himself properly, a stupid accident with a cart, and everything had to stop.

The doctor who came to see his crushed leg noticed her at once, though he said nothing. He went home with his heart pounding and sat that evening in his study with the latest transactions of the local archaeological society, unable to concentrate. When his housekeeper came in with his supper he felt oddly ashamed and made an extra effort to chat. After a couple of days he went back to the farm and found his patient, though in considerable pain from his leg, extraordinarily calm. My head, he said. My head is clear. The doctor sat on a chair near the bed and asked tactful questions about the war, glancing across at Anaig, peeling vegetables at the table, to make sure he made no mistakes. She did not look up much, but nodded her head.

In the semi-darkness behind him he could feel the statue. Entering the house for a second time his eyes had found her clear, astonishing face, fulfilling the promise of his memory.

She stood just behind his right shoulder, standing on a blanket chest against the wall. He examined the man's leg again, carefully, and changed the dressing, gritted against the necessary jolts of his patient's pain. Once the man was settled back in the bed the doctor stood and talked to them both from the hearth, from where he could see the statue better. The curve of a cheek. Adrenalin made him bright. He was courteous and sympathetic as though at some social function, drawing his listeners out of themselves until all three of them were at ease. Children played around him. He went home that night full of desire, happy.

On the third visit he asked about her. As he had expected, the man was reluctant to talk at first, but the doctor spoke generally of his interest in old things and told him of his own finds, a handful of silver coins and bits of pot, the broken sword on his mantlepiece. He said he thought the statue had been left by the same people who buried the little coins. As he spoke his thin hands moved softly in the air around her, outlining her head and neck, stroking along the rounded childish arms without touching her. Eventually the man told him about the field and finding the swan, and how he had waited the length of the war to come back and dig her free. He had fixed the head, arms and feet to the torso with joints of wood; the long fragile robe was crumbling slightly even as he dug her up, the metal of it had been beaten so fine. Like cigarette paper, he said, rubbing his thumb and forefinger together. The doctor saw how well he had made the pieces hold together and complimented him. I used to do a lot of things with wood, said the man. Anaig gestured to the youngest child, sitting in a heap of wooden animals, a cart, a doll.

At the next visit the doctor persuaded them to let the eldest child show him the field. The place was easy enough to spot, since it had never been cultivated; a small half-ring of stones marked it off. He bent excitedly and scraped down to the clay, then climbed up on the bank and looked around him in all directions. The wind caught his coat-tails. He smiled down at the boy who watched him in silence, and told him to come up. With a hand on the boy's shoulder and the other waving his hat in appropriate directions he outlined ditches and ramparts around them, lit beacons on neighbouring hills, drew lines of roads with soldiers marching and conjured a fleet out to sea; the boy was mesmerised by this revelation of the past in his own landscape. As they set off down the hill in the rain the doctor gave him a coin. He handed it over to his mother, but kept the vision to himself.

After that the doctor simply waited, knowing it would happen in time. For the first three or four weeks the family lived a period of readjustment, with all the old patterns of their previous life dissolved. The man on the bed talked to his children; he drew for them, and carved. When the pain in his leg was too much he became short-tempered, but there were no more silences or weeping. Neighbours brought food. Anaig took in extra washing, the doctor himself would judiciously accept a meal in lieu of payment. For a while there was a buoyancy, a sense of surplus.

But as the gift of a clear head became something he took for granted the man became anxious about the future. Anaig was tired, and growing tight-lipped. His fields were uncared for. The doctor felt the mood in the house change, and noted the progress of their anxiety with pity and satisfaction. Still he waited, gently deflecting the man's questions about his leg until he was sure they had no choice. He came finally one evening in February, stamping his feet and shaking water from his overcoat. He stood as usual in front of the fire, keeping his eyes away from the statue and the restless shadow of the swan which flickered against the wall.

The leg, he told them, would always be useless. There was no question of taking up active farm work again. The pain would probably go, but the leg itself would never work. The man on the bed turned his face to the wall. Anaig sat looking blank. If they would forgive him, the doctor continued, for discussing the subject, he realised the difficulties they were in, and he wanted to help. He thought of it as a business proposition, he said, a deal between friends. It would benefit them all.

He was intelligent enough to understand the flash of rage in his patient's eyes as he accepted. It was indeed too good a solution for them to refuse, offering as it did a new start with no loss of dignity. The barn would be renovated and converted to a workshop; tools were to be bought, as were the first few consignments of wood. There would be some financial help in the first three years, to be repaid over a long time; he would, of course, recommend them to his other clients. So the farmer became a carpenter and the doctor got the statue.

She stared across his study out past the apple tree to the distant, mostly invisible, sea. He sometimes lifted his head from his writing to smile at her, or stand in front of her intently waiting for thoughts to formulate before going back to his writing, flexing his thin fingers against the cold. He continued to give talks to his local antiquarian society, to publish in archaeological journals, to pursue his theory of an organised and complex gallo-roman resistance to invasion. In the landscape around him he saw defences, hiding places, battle sites and holy places warding off the threat from the sea. In none of his publications, and to none of his antiquarian friends, did he ever mention the bronze goddess.

There was another war, and this time it came to them. It shook him deeply to watch his imagined embattled landscape come suddenly real; to look out to sea in fear. Seeing far enough ahead to imagine the presence of foreign troops in his village he was ready long before his neighbours had realised what would happen. He hid his most valuable books in the cellar and buried the statue in the garden somewhere near the apple tree before leaving his house and housekeeper to the imminent arrivals and disappearing off to join the Resistance.

At the beginning, crouching in wet leaves behind a wall or hunched exhausted in a sunken lane of beech trees and muddy hoof marks it would seem to him to make sense. That war came round in cycles like the turning sky, turning randomness into patterns over the course of centuries. That people, races, did not change their fundamental configurations any more than the stars did. That history could predict, with great exactitude, the conflicts of future generations. That he had seen it coming, and had aligned himself with his people against the enemy. Only later, much later, as an old man, he was forced to admit to himself that it had not really been that clear. There were certain days, usually in July and August, when he would be obliged to close up the shutters and stay indoors reading, with lights on if necessary, to block out scenes triggered by the heat and the glare.

They had arrived at the chosen farm singly but more or less at the same time, sweating and sick with heat. Too thirsty for courtesy they brushed past the old woman in the doorway who had been reluctant to let them in. They had passed a large jug of water around the table while he explained, since his companions did not speak Breton, a simplied version of what they had come to do. Food and rest for two nights, he said. We are on important business. But the daughter, a tall bony woman with two small children, looked straight at him. Your sort are trouble, she said. We don't want your sort here. It was a shock to him to hear this, and he glossed a little in his translation. They all agreed that there was nothing for it but to stay.

The following day at midday they were eating at the big table. They had been out all night, returning before dawn for some sleep. The older woman and her daughter served them silently. He had given up trying to explain that they were on the same side and was silently cursing them for their obtuseness when the door shook under a volley of blows. The old woman cried out. The seated men rose in confusion to face the soldiers and their guns. There was a frozen silence of one, two seconds, and then one of the doctor's companions, a young man, panicked. As the German soldiers coolly motioned for the men to put up their hands he grabbed the daughter by her arm and pulled her in front of him, reaching for his gun. *Ma Doue*, she said, her face ugly with terror. *Ma Doue*. The doctor shouted at him and scrambled behind the table for protection, pulling the two children with him. There were a couple of shots and the young man cried in pain; they pulled the frozen woman to one side and shot him dead. Then they moved in, rounding up the two other men from the corner where they crouched and ordering them out of the front door. As the doctor passed the older woman she spat, and called them cowards.

When, a year or so later, he returned to his house, it had been done over, smashed and stripped. The housekeeper had gone. He did not look for her or get anyone to replace her. Instead he spent weeks cleaning the place himself, room by room, washing and painting the floors and walls and throwing away torn and soiled cushions, curtains, mouldy rugs and broken cups and vases without replacing them, so that it shone bare and white. In his study, where many of the books and papers still seemed to be intact, he took down volumes to remove the layers of dust and washed down the wide shelves, repainting the dark oak panelling white. Once the study was ready he went out into his overgrown garden to dig up the statue.

The garden was unrecognisable under bramble and dock. The nettles reached his thighs. He hacked a space round the apple tree and began to tear up roots and dig at the soil underneath. It took him several attempts to find her. He had wrapped her in velvet, then hessian sacking and oilcloth and it was this that he finally pulled, damp and lumpen from the ground. He laid it down carefully, like a sick child, on the cleared space beside him and cut the string. Unrolling it his hands told him something was wrong, and as the last layer of cloth unfolded he saw with horror that the entire body of the statue, the long beaten-metal robe, fine as cigarette paper, had disintegrated. Guilt and grief overwhelmed him. He caught up the cloth with the pieces in it and ran into the house. There he laid her out on the polished walnut table like a broken doll: a pair of sandalled feet, two rounded arms, and the terrifying, clear-faced, helmeted head.

Tethered Angel

I used to really like the trips into town with Nain until her chapel burned down and they moved the angel. I got milkshake in the Penguin and a football magazine for my trouble, and all I had to do was carry a few bags, listen a lot and talk a bit as we inched round town. She's so big and heavy she can't go fast and on Saturdays, with all the people, it's like a slow-motion war, murderous three-wheeler buggies coming at us out of the crowd and whole families forced to break round her, a huge floral rock. The beaten-up tartan trolley gets a few shins every time. The trolley is her excuse for sending me up, of course, because she couldn't hike it up the stairs and the only time we went together the tiny lift got stuck with us in it and she said *byth eto*, never again, not even for him.

Now, Lewis John, she says, scooping the last of the pale clingy froth from the bottom of her coffee cup and watching too closely as I eat the last of my iced bun, we'll go to Boots, she says, and my heart cringes like a snail. Outside Boots she tells me, as she has told me many times before, that I don't want to traipse round after her looking for face cream, so will I save her legs and run up next door to check on him? Yes, Nain, I will. And in she goes, filling the tiny aisles, banging her horrible trolley against people's legs and reversing into stands where two-for-one suncreams sit in precarious displays. You would think that anyone would gladly exchange such embarassment for a quiet ten minutes in the town museum, with its shop full of retro toys – pop-guns and wooden swords, knot-puzzles and glow-in-the-dark ducks, metal chickens and wacky historical tea-towels, mini-toolkits and key-ring torches and other wonders, many of which I now own, for reasons which will become clear. The museum itself also goes out of its way to be child-friendly; for those who don't get that excited by old agricultural implements and chamber pots there might be a display of old model cars or lead soldiers; and there are skulls and things, fossils, if you go and look.

Which is all fine if that's what you're there for, but I'm not. I have to go and check on the angel. Unsurprisingly, he is where I left him last week, tied to a pillar at the far end of the main gallery, still clutching his cumbersome armful of bronze palm fronds and still balanced with one foot on a small bronze beach ball inscribed with the names of the war dead. Over the many weeks that I have had this job I have perfected the art of checking him over while walking past and pretending to be looking for something else; it takes me about half a minute, including a double check of the singed wing, as Nain insists. The damaged patch has been roughened by the fire, a weird blend of colours run together, reddish-brown, black, and an oxidised pale green. If the man on the desk is watching I tend to head deliberately back to the shop area and buy an item from the 50p pile to prove that I'm not shoplifting. I now have a collection of things from there that I don't really want, though I sometimes use them to bribe my sister, so the money isn't entirely wasted. If they're busy at the counter I can get away with looking for an imaginary birthday present and then shaking my head and making for the stairs. I go down them two at a time and wait for Nain to come crashing out of Boots. Well, Lewis John, she says, how was he today?

Tethered Angel

Bronze angels, especially those under cover, age incredibly slowly, and so there is very little, in fact, that I can tell her. I mostly stick to a version of he was looking fine, and vary it occasionally by adding that someone – an elderly man, or a young mum with a baby in a sling – went over to have a closer look while I was there. Sometimes, of course, I have to make these people up. Today the museum was emptier than ever; all the visitors must have been on the beach. This made my task more painful, and I think it was because I was feeling even more miserably self-conscious than normal that it took me a minute to realise that, for once, something really had changed. And then another minute to realise what it was.

When he first arrived at the museum he was tethered to the post by his ankle, the one still in the air. They used one of those adjustable straps with a clip-down metal buckle, like the straps people put round suitcases – once round the post and then tight round his ankle, as if to dissuade him from lifting off again. He has quite thin legs, like me, and is about my size, though being an angel you have to assume he is a lot older than eleven, several thousand years older in fact. His hands are much bigger than mine. And of course he looks a lot more like a girl. What I couldn't see at first and then saw with a slight shock was that they'd moved the strap: he wasn't held by the ankle anymore, he was properly restrained with a new black strap around his chest. It went under his arm-pits and under his wings and round the pillar. It was quite well hidden by those palm fronds but once you'd seen it you would find it hard to ignore.

Nain was devastated. *Be mae o wedi 'neud?* she said, standing like a huge wreck on the pavement while the crowds surged round her. *What has he done?*

I managed to manoeuvre her a few hundred yards to the prom, and we sat down until her agitation had calmed enough for me to suggest an ice cream; I thought that the sinfulness of the treat might distract her. But even sat there licking a mint-choc-chip she succeeded in being tragic, and as I couldn't really answer her questions I just looked at people, and out across the blue sea, and tried to be silent and comforting.

After a while, when we'd finished our ice creams, I said, are we going home now? She looked out to sea and shook her head. A bit more shopping then? No, she said, no, Lewis John, we've got to go back and find out what happened.

Nothing happened, Nain. They've moved the strap, is all.

But why? she said, looking suddenly very determined. I felt a faint panic washing over me, cold as seawater.

Safety, I said. Health and Safety. Perhaps they were worried he might tip.

Tip? she said, incredulous. Tip? Him?

And she hauled herself up, breathing heavily. *No Nain. No. Please, Nain, no.*

I'm not sure the lift is working properly yet, I said, helpless. We'll go and see.

She was sweetness itself to the lady downstairs. Asked if she'd mind keeping an eye on the trolley while she popped upstairs a moment, and got her to check that the tiny lift was operational. Hope draining away, I squeezed in with her and crossed my fingers for a dramatic mid-flight breakdown or a nicely jammed door, but the door slid open first time and we emerged like something coming out of a can into the calm brown air of the agricultural section. She didn't even make her joke about old crocks, just headed for the main gallery, walking quicker than I knew she could. I hated the sound of her breathing in the stillness. *Don't go to the desk.*

I saw, in a glance, that it was as bad as it could be. The man at the desk was the one who peered at me, who made me feel like a shoplifter. There were more people around than earlier, and among them, in the shop with her parents, a girl from my year at school. I tugged gently at Nain's arm. Come and see him first, I said. Before you say anything. You can see that he's not hurt. He's fine really. Look.

She hadn't been up since that first time, about six months before. She'd cried a lot then, and stroked the singed wing, and when the gentle curator, not the sarcastic one, had come over to ask her not to touch he'd been so taken aback that he'd gone and got her a cup of tea from the machine, and talked to her about the chapel and its history, and listened patiently to her theory about how the arson was all planned by the Developers so they could knock half the town down with it. I had disappeared to look at fossils, which was stupid, I realised afterwards, because more people might have recognised me when I came up on my own after that and I wouldn't have felt so awkward.

Now here she was again, not crying this time, but full of indignation, puffed out with it like an opera singer.

That wing's no better, she said angrily, glaring. It's hardly healed at all.

I had no answer to that.

And the strap, the black strap that bound him to the white pillar with its wedding cake cornice, was more than she could bear. How dare they? she said, nearly choking, How dare they? *O Duw, sut allen nhw?* He can hardly breathe. And she reached up into the rigid palm fronds towards the buckle. I was utterly focused on keeping my back to the man at the desk and the girl from my year, and I could only wait, sickening, for the polite voice ringing across the gallery, *Excuse me madam, would you mind not touching the…*? And then, in a terrible explosion of wrath, it would be Judgement Day.

Hello again, said a friendly voice just behind me. She turned round, red in the face, still puffing.

Come to check up on him? He smiled. We've been looking after him for you.

She couldn't smile back, but at least she didn't shout.

If you are looking after him, she said very deliberately, then why have you done this?

The strap? he looked puzzled, and glanced at me. Oh, Health and Safety, you know what it's like. I suppose it does look a bit, um, incongruous.

She stared at him in complete disbelief. Then, even more slowly, hissing each *s* with restrained fury:

It is *diss-ress-pect*.

This time the gentle curator was even more taken aback, but he thought quickly, intelligently, and, with another glance at me, hoping perhaps for some complicity I was too frozen or too young to give him, he came slowly forward and, putting one hand on her arm, reached up past her with the other.

In that case, he said quietly and carefully, his fingers feeling for the buckle, in that case, let me help you with this.

Lancaut

Let the curve of an uncrossable river hug me; let the high wooded cliffs wrap me around. Give me no views, no prospects, no bloody sunsets staining the dark sea, no rolling hills, no spires or distant cattle in morning mist, no challenging, far-off peaks, no perspective. I am up against it, walled in, caught in the river's slowly tightening noose. Lancaut, Lancaut, only one way out. And that involves back-tracking, never a good idea, up the lane, through the woods, past the church and the expensive cluster of houses to the big road, a real road, with Tescos five minutes up and the horses ten minutes down. Not that I will be needing them again. The horses, that is.

Our house, our home, is more or less the last one standing in what was never quite a village on a comma of land by the Wye. I did, briefly, toy with the idea of buying Piercefield itself in the interests of poetic justice; money from the racecourse in the grounds recovering the wreck. But then we found this, more our size, and had it beautifully renovated, mostly eighteenth-century, goldish stone. Two fields slope down to the loop of the river, we are almost islanded, what a place to find, my love, what a place. And what a place to leave me, what were you thinking of? All winter long we worked closely with the heritage people, employed the architects they recommended, employed the

105

builder they recommended: dark, broadshouldered, with dancing eyes and a feel for stone and women. And what a fantastic job he did.

So I see no one much except the postman, and occasionally the people from the Nature Reserve, very keen they are, plying me with leaflets. And weekends it gets quite busy with walkers; I must get a sign made to point them back to the path, I don't like their nervous circlings around the house. During the day I go through all the legal stuff as carefully as I can, a page at a time, because almost the only thing I care about now is that she should not get her hands on the money. I start drinking around four, and spend the evenings crying and watching television.

Sometimes I walk. Down through the fields to pick up the path along the riverbank; left towards the ruins of St James' chapel; right round to Ban-y-Gor woods. A circular walk would no doubt be more satisfying, but appears to involve scrambling up a mud path to the ridge and cutting down through the trees on the other side and I have no energy for that, so I tend to just turn round after a bit and retrace my steps. Which could feel like defeat, but I always feel less bitter after a walk. Sometimes, then, I cook.

Yesterday I went left. It drizzled a bit, but the sun kept getting through, lighting clumps of celandine and bright green moss. I felt muffled with my hood up and pulled it down to find that light rain, properly approached, can be rather pleasant. It was a Wednesday and there was no one at all around until I got level with the chapel, where I caught sight of a figure inside the walls and decided to carry along the river path to avoid a conversation. About twenty minutes upriver I reached the point marked on the leaflet as the site of an old Roman bridge. Not uncrossable after all, I thought, not to them. I stood and looked at the low-tide stretches of grey-brown mud and thought about damp Romans tramping back and forth until I felt exhausted. I turned back; the weather was closing in.

Bastard still there, I thought morosely, seeing the figure again apparently inspecting the wall nearest the path. I put my hood back up, my hands in my pockets, and braced myself to return a cheery hello with a terminal sideways nod.

Disconcertingly, the man is sitting on the wall dressed like a monk.

He raises a hand in blessing as I attempt to stride by and calls my name out very softly. Which pulls me up short, of course.

I'm sorry? I say, with just a quiver of threat in my voice.

Don't be, says the man.

I stop and face him now, and pull my hood down again for a better look. It is raining with some conviction, and the effect is to make him look oddly blurred. I must, I think, have heard him wrong.

And you are – I wave a sarcastic hand at the ruined chapel – St James, I presume?

He looks annoyed. Of course not, he says, James never came near the place. It's always been me here, since the beginning.

Right, I say, the light dawning. Well, it's a dreadful day for it. There'll be more around at the weekend; families and dogwalkers and ramblers and all sorts. Didn't they give you a brolly?

Poor sod, I think, and start to move on. Bet they pay him eff-all as well.

I don't need one, he calls after me, and blesses me again.

At the stile I look back to see if he is still sitting on the wall. He isn't.

A few days later I saw him again. The valley was a different place, all cleansed and radiant with March sunshine and birdsong and I had just had a brainwave and was putting it into action. The bedroom, where I rarely sleep, preferring to pass out painlessly on the sofa, was, I decided, a poisoned well at the heart of my house. Clean it, I thought. Purge it. Keep nothing. Oxfam the lot. So I skinned the duvet of its creamy lace cover, and stripped the pillows and cushions of all their frills and stuffed them into black bin bags. And there I was balanced on a chintzy stool awkwardly unhooking chintzy curtains in the big bay window when I saw him, still in his monk's costume, down on the riverpath at the bottom of the field, head bent, hands clasped behind his back, tonsure shining in the sun. I left the curtain hanging on for dear life and went out through the back door, picking up a leaflet as I left. I wave it briskly as I catch him up.

It's Kiw-id , isn't it? I say.

No. No it isn't, he says, wincing visibly.

But it says here, I say. It says here that the early Welsh saint Kiw-id gives his name to the valley: Lan-Caut. Though how that works I admit I have no idea. Look. I flash the leaflet under his thin nose.

I know. It is me, yes, but you're saying it wrong, it's Cewydd.
?

Try *Qué*

Qué

Now *with*, as in with.

With.

Cewydd

Qué-with. I'm no good at languages, I say, I could always call you Caut.

You could not, he says. Try again.

Qué-with.

Better.

Thanks. Nicer day for working, isn't it? Do you really have to wear sandals in this mud?

I wasn't working, particularly, he says.

No? Well. Nice anyway. I gesture proprietorially at the pale cliff face opposite. Even this looks different today, and God knows I've done enough looking.

It's different every day, he says, you'd be surprised at how much changes in a year, never mind a thousand.

A thousand and a half, I correct him, checking my leaflet. AD 625 you're supposed to be first recorded, remember.

No supposed about it, he says, with just a flicker of wounded pride.

I grin. I rather like this man.

You've really found your vocation, haven't you?

I have. Indeed.

He courteously turns down the offer of a cup of coffee, wishes me well with the purging, and continues along the tight inside curve of the river to the woods behind. Today, I think, he looks not so much blurred as translucent. Wye valley light, the despair of generations of watercolourists, is a marvellous thing.

That bright interlude was the last for a while. Rain set in, the wind came whipping irritably around the house and flinging hail in rough fistfuls at the windows. I succumbed to a stinking head-cold, lost my energy and all will to move. I drank more than ever, kept the television on all the time, and felt foul and stupid. I craved fresh orange juice but knew I was too drunk and too weak to face the drive to Tescos. I wasn't even sure I had enough petrol to get there.

One evening as I was feeding bits of the neatly chopped-up bed into my state-of-the-art wood-burner there came an unmistakable tapping on the living-room window. I tugged the curtain back slightly to find Cewydd's pale face peering grotesquely in at me. I gestured him round to the back door and went to unlock it. He was dripping wet and shivering. I looked hard at the kitchen clock and out into the dark to make sure.

It's night, I said, with some confidence.

It is.

And it's pissing down.

It is.

Right. I looked at him. He was still in his monk's costume, but now, at least, he had added a grey woollen cloak with a hood. I gradually, fuzzily, realised that my friend probably didn't work for the Lancaut Trust after all. An obsessive, then, an enthusiast. A loony in my living room. Oh what the hell, I thought. Who am I to judge. I like him.

Um, I said. You'd better come and warm up then.

Thank you, John. You don't look too well.

You and me both, I said. Let me get you a cup of tea.

Don't worry, he said, I don't need anything. I came to see how you were, really.

Tea, I said firmly. Or whisky. Sit down: you can watch the bed burn for me.

I'll do that, he said, and gladly.

When I come in with the tray he has taken his cloak off and is just poking another bit of headboard into the stove. The firelight does strange things to his face, making it glow as if from the inside. He looks up with a big smile and I see for the first time what a curious grey-green his eyes are.

Excellent. He rubs thin fingers. I haven't seen a proper fire for ages.

Where do you live? I ask him, putting the stuff down with a clank. Did you really walk through this or have you left the car at the top?

Walked up from the chapel, he says simply. You know I did. Tea?

No.

Whisky?

I don't think so. It smells nice, though.

What do you eat?

Oh not much. Cress. Spring water. I don't need a lot.

At this point I give up asking questions and sink back into the sofa, where I drink all the tea and most of the whisky and tell him the sorry details of my life to date.

Sex and money, I say grimly. Nothing but trouble.

Cewydd nods sympathetically. They are inherently sinful,

he says. They draw the mind away from its true object of contemplation.

Which is? I say stupidly.

God, says Cewydd smugly, and smiles into the fire.

Having no god, nor any inclination to acquire one, I drag the subject away from my own misery. Tell me about the good old days, I say, back in the sixth century. You didn't come here alone? No Mrs Cewydd then?

Monastic order, he says. Don't be daft.

And he sketches for me an idyll of monks fishing and farming peacefully on the little peninsula, and though chunks of it sound as though they have floated wholesale out of the Lancaut leaflet I am too tired to check up and let him go on.

I do miss the salmon, he says, sadly. Thirty-seven years since I caught a salmon here.

Nuts and berries, I say, sleepily.

Plenty, he says. And herbs, we cultivated all kinds of things. If you're still a mess come June I'll prepare you some St John's wort, if I can still find it.

Elecampane, I say, even more sleepily. Leaflet says found up top, very rare, import.

Planted it myself, says Cewydd. Up on the Spital Meend. Good for lepers.

At some point he gets up to see to the fire, and I'm sure I can see the glow of it right through him.

When I woke the next morning with a clear head and no sore throat and a fine spring day nudging its way through the crack in the curtains I knew it was a miracle. I had a shower, changed my clothes, and stood tall. Then I drove to Tescos on a thimbleful of petrol and sliced my way through the Saturday crowds like a hot knife through butter, like a spear singing in the blue air. I stocked up on honeyed ham, French-style bread and litres of freshly squeezed orange juice. I also bought a packet of organic watercress and a bottle of Tŷ Nant.

For the next two or three walks, when I was actively out looking for him, he didn't show. I even did the strenuous circular, and found myself admiring the white haze of wood anemones and actively looking forward to the blue haze of bluebells. But I am still as tidal as the river, and so it was inevitable that he should turn up on a bad day, a day full of lawyers' wranglings and angry flashbacks, a cliff-face, mudflats, hopeless day. I was sitting at the big kitchen table with a beer and a packet of crisps and a pile of solicitors' letters when he walked in.

Even revenge is depressing, I say, not looking up. And complicated. There must be simpler ways.

He says nothing, but sits down at the table opposite me.

I bet it wasn't like this in the sixth century.

Legal stuff doesn't change, he says. It's all about how many cows and the length of silver rods, no one understands it really.

But saints are above all that, aren't they? There are quicker ways of punishing people, surely? What did you do?

About what?

You know, enemies; people out to get you. Infidels. Landgrabbers. People nicking your salmon.

Oh. Curse them.

I've done that, I say. What else?

He looks thoughtful.

Melt them.

I look up. What do you...? Oh. You mean metaphorically? As in soften their anger, dissolve their rage?

No. Metaphors are inherently sinful. They draw the mind away from its rightful object of contemplation.

Bollocks.

Precisely.

He reaches for a crisp but thinks better of it. I remember the cress and go to the fridge. The bag opens with a pop and releases a fetid slimy smell.

I'm sorry, I say. There's water somewhere for you.

I'm fine.

I back-track. But you melted them. Your enemies. Really?

Mm-mm.

He is trying very hard to sound casual, I think. I allow myself a minute or two to picture her melted on the spot, in various settings, with and without her man, but begin to have some difficulty with the details.

Do they turn into a pool? I ask. A pool of flesh? Or water? Or do they soak into the ground? How does it work?

He stares impenetrably into the middle distance; then shrugs.

I can't remember, he says. That part isn't important.

I don't think you've ever done it, I say unkindly. You're such a fraud. You can't remember anything that isn't on the leaflet, why's that, I wonder?

It's the dark ages, he says defensively. They're shrouded in mystery. I honestly can't remember everything, it was a long time ago.

But I'm still needling, still wanting to hurt.

You're pathetic. I bet you forgive your enemies at the last minute every time, like a true Christian. Proper saint, you are.

Lord, I sound like my Gran.

Proper saint I am, says Cewydd stiffly, and gets up from the table and strides out of the back door and down the field, thinning as he goes. I watch through the window. By the time he reaches the path there is nothing, no one there. I fetch myself another beer to prove that I won, and sit back down with my cursed letters.

But it has been such a long time since I last raised my voice in anger at another human being that even a tiff with a touchy dark-age saint upsets my pitiful concentration beyond all recall and it is not long before I am down by the river looking for him, clutching the blue bottle of Tŷ Nant.

I clear my throat and glance around for dog walkers.

Cewydd!!

The river has filled again with the tide from the sea and a rich harvest of rain from up in the Welsh hills. I don't know if it's best to go upstream or down.

Cewydd!!

The curved white cliff looms. My small voice bounces off it.

Cewydd, I'm sorry!

This is ridiculous. I feel like weeping. And then my little call is answered by another voice, a huge voice, metallic, nasal, rhythmical, familiar, coming over the cliff above me from the grounds at Piercefield, filling the theatre of Lancaut. I am awestruck. It is the three-thirty from Chepstow carried on the rainwashed air. Magnified. Liturgical. The words are completely unintelligible but I know their rhythms like the Lord's Prayer. I close my eyes and feel them galloping in my blood. And then there is Cewydd standing beside me, as rapt as I am. I ceremoniously hand him the spring-water and watch with a smile as he holds the unbelievable blue glass bottle reverently and incredulously up to the light, overwhelmed by its blueness, reaching out towards the voice of god.

The Hostage

He was glad, being tired and still angry, to find the place so tractable to cliché. He did the little harbour and the fishing boats that keeled over on the weed at low tide, he did the boulders of pinkish granite and the yellowing bracken, the gorse and the gulls. Then he moved up to the village and did the neat twisting streets of stonebuilt houses, the fifteenth-century church with its enclosure, its calvary, the smell of the old-fashioned *épicérie* and the fishermen lined up at the counter in the Bar-des-Sports where he sat with his notebook and a beer. In the interests of balance he included the ugly new *mairie*, the sprawling campsite and the vulgar white villas spreading along both arms of the bay, the private islands, the big yachts anchored out to sea. Everything slipped into place. He read it through and finished his beer, then thoughtfully added the budgerigars, about a dozen of them, in separate cages, hung from pegs sticking randomly out of the far wall. He swapped the heap of receipts for a pile of ten-franc pieces and went out, nodding towards the bar.

They didn't nod back, but they watched him go. He knew the air ruffled by his leaving would settle down more comfortably without him. He felt in his jacket for the cigarette he had rolled earlier, failed to get a light from his plastic lighter, felt uselessly for matches and gave up. Easier to go without than break it all up again in there. He walked slowly back to his hotel, stopping in the square to phone his office, then Sylvie. Someone had left a thin book of matches on top of the phone.

The next morning he began proper work, patiently making conversation. From the patronne at the hotel, and the sharp-faced woman at the baker's, he found out where the boy's mother lived, that she had practically withdrawn from the village. A cousin did all her shopping and brought them regular bulletins. That she had gone to church, though she didn't speak to anyone after the mass and it was impossible even to catch her eye. He needn't bother trying to visit her at the house, she didn't answer the door; the cousin let herself in with a key. Or the telephone. He knew about the telephone.

He went back to the cafe, made a few notes, and sat for a while reading the local paper. With his second coffee he bought a national newspaper and turned straight to his own piece in the middle; he read it through casually, then folded the paper back to the front page, setting it down in front of him while he lit a cigarette. From the layout, without reading a word, he could see that nothing had changed. They had shifted the picture to make room for an earthquake, and the young soldier's blurred white face with its dark eyes was now in the right hand corner flanked by a thinnish column of words. He succumbed for a moment to the fascination of the forty-eight-hour deadline, or however many hours it was now; to the peculiar bloated nature of the present, with everyone moving slowly, deliberately, inside it, as if on the moon. Most of Saturday left, and the whole of Sunday. He slid his mind away out of trouble with a small, well-practised effort, left the paper lying and headed towards the house, hoping to intercept the cousin.

He followed a lane out of the village away from the sea, walking quickly up the hill, faintly thrilled to be feeling purposeful again, and lifted by the smell of damp bracken, the blackberries, the light. This was childhood stuff for him, he had a Breton grandmother, there had been a few memorable summers before she died. He had been very young; the family never went back after. Something frightening happened, an accident or an argument, he wasn't sure now which. He turned down a cart track and picked his way round patches of wet mud, stopping near a cluster of elder trees growing by a spring within sight of the house. He leaned against a wall, watching the door, picking dark beads off the tree and flicking them into the small dark pool. He felt or imagined a hostility from the house. The door was shut. His mind dredged up some vague recognition of the unspoken country rule that was supposed to keep such doors open at all times. After five minutes he went up to the door and knocked.

When nothing happened after several attempts he began to walk slowly round the house, peering into windows. She was in the kitchen, peeling potatoes at the table and staring at the television. He watched her from behind, trying to see her face; her hands worked steadily, the peel curling into piles which she swept to one side, but she hardly moved her head. Beyond her he saw the brash graphics of the lunchtime news. The black and white photo flashed up onto the screen, flashed away. The woman carried on peeling, bone white potatoes piling up underwater in a huge perspex bowl, far too many of them for one person, or even two.

His stomach retracted with a kind of shame, or fear; stage-fright, he thought, get on with it. Shifting from the edge of the window he stood in full view, waiting to catch her eye. He had to wait a while, but when the news came to an end she put down her knife and a half-peeled potato and went over to the television. He glanced at his watch and realised as she pressed the buttons on the old-fashioned set that she had changed channels to get the news all over again. Braced to meet her gaze as she turned back, he coughed and moved his hand in a friendly gesture, smiling a friendly smile. She stopped at the corner of the table, wiping her hands on her overall. She had seen him, but her face registered no surprise. He smiled again and she looked at him, completely expressionless, a little tired, before turning and sitting back down to her task. He tapped on the window like a fool. Then he gave up.

The cousin was a short, broad woman with red cheeks and a basin haircut; she looked like a friendly monk. He met her in the lane, loaded with bags, and stopped her to ask the way back to the village. She opened up like a daisy. She was going back to her cousin, he had heard about the boy, yes? His mother, that's right, in a terrible way, she had awful trouble getting her to eat, and as for speaking, it was like living with a stone. She went in two or three times a day, she did, to keep her company, but she never said a word, not one. Her accent was thick as butter. He was hugely encouraged. He'd been hoping, he said, to see the lady herself; he had tried at the house but wondered if, perhaps, he could just join them both for five minutes? She threw him a charming smile and said he was wasting his time. No one, except the priest, got into that house any more. She picked up her heavy bags and laughed at him sweetly when he offered to help. She was fine, she said, couldn't he see she was built like an ox? He tried to insist, his chance slipping away, but her cheerfulness was impregnable and before he knew it she was halfway up the muddy track, ploughing through the puddles.

He cursed himself and got out a cigarette. He used to be able to get in anywhere. He smoked bitterly until he had relaxed enough to realise that it really didn't matter; he had more than enough. A few words with the priest and he would be all but done. Another easy piece: a mother's anxious wait, predictable in its contours and easily assembled with the help of the cheerful cousin. He scribbled down a couple of her phrases, holding his notebook awkwardly in the middle of the muddy path. Then he headed back to the village.

The priest was unavailable all afternoon; visiting the sick, he supposed. So he spent the time back at the cafe. It was sunny enough to sit outside with a beer and the local newspaper. The local correspondent had clearly had no better luck than himself, he saw; though there was a useful quote from the priest which he could borrow if necessary. When the football started, he moved inside with the other men. They still didn't like him. But they were polite, and as the game progressed they relaxed back into Breton. Some of the younger ones would have gone to school with him, he thought. He watched their faces carefully during the news bulletins, and saw solemnity and fascination; a couple of the older men swore and turned away. He did not have the energy to go and work at them. He went back to the hotel and sat down with a full packet of cigarettes and a whisky to knock up his next piece.

It was unexpectedly difficult, and when he had finished he disliked it. But he could not bear to begin again, so he rolled the paper into a belligerent baton and went out to the phone box in the square, where he phoned it through to the office in a voice of tired defiance. Then he phoned Sylvie, though he knew, because she had told him, that she had gone out for a drink with her radio friends. He thought of her tapping her nails on the bar and crossing her beautiful legs, and left a sulky message on her answerphone. He hung up miserable, rang again with an apology, and then walked down towards the sea, dropping his torn-up script into a convenient bin.

The tide was out somewhere in the dark; he could smell the weed. He followed the coast road away from the village for about twenty minutes, looking mostly at his feet, turning at last to retrace his steps when he remembered his cigarettes back in the hotel room. As he re-entered the village, which looked suddenly strange, he noticed lights in the vicarage.

The priest opened the door blinking a little behind spectacles but did not look surprised. He was polite and relaxed.

'What can I do for you?' he said.

'My name is Paul Lecros.' He hesitated. 'I'm a journalist.' And again, apologetic, 'I am not religious.'

The priest smiled wryly and stood aside to let him in. 'I won't hold it against you.'

The room had a small fire and walls of books; a huge desk at the window was covered in more books and papers, which shone under a bright lamp. 'I'm sorry,' said Paul, 'I've interrupted your work.'

'It doesn't matter,' said the older man, and took off his spectacles to rub his eyes. Then he leaned over and pulled a curtain across the window which looked out towards the dark sea. 'I always forget to draw it. And anyway, I like the lighthouses. Did you see them?' He hadn't.

They sat in chairs either side of the fire. 'What can I do for you?' said the priest. 'I've come,' said Paul, 'about the hostage's mother.' The other man nodded, said nothing. 'And I'm not sure why I've come, because I've finished the piece I was going to use you in and it's all phoned through so I couldn't change it if I wanted to. I saw her in the house with the television on, but I couldn't speak to her; they tell me you can. I suppose it's because I could do with a couple of details for tomorrow. I suppose that's why I'm here.'

The priest looked thoughtful, and said nothing. Paul carried on, perfectly aware of what he was doing to himself, unable to stop. 'I could have done them myself, the details; I probably would have, but your light was on. So make it easier for me: tell me how she suffers, and how she finds support in God, and how you see your role as her guide in this difficult time… I'm sorry, I didn't mean to be rude. I don't doubt your support for her, I don't begrudge her her faith; Christ, at a time like this, what else is there? I'm sorry.'

'There's no need.' said the priest. 'Shall we have a drink?'

He went to a glass cabinet and got out whisky and glasses. Paul felt helplessly grateful, and began to explain himself and apologise all over again, but the older man stopped him.

'I know exactly what it is you want,' he said, 'and I would even give it to you if I could. I have some respect for your newspaper clichés; I think they serve a purpose – at the very least, they help organise emotions. But I'm afraid I can't give you even an approximation of what you're after.' He sipped his whisky and gave a sort of shrug. 'I'm no support to her. She doesn't talk to me either. I'm not quite sure why she lets me in – why she lets Marivonne let me in, rather. I go every day, for about an hour, and Marivonne makes me coffee; I sit at the kitchen table and talk as gently as I can, as if I were talking to myself, thinking out loud. About pain, and patience, and God in all of that, of course.'

'The television…'

'Yes, it's on all the time. Did you know it's just pictures, no sound?'

'Even the news?'

'Yes, everything; just those ghastly pictures. She doen't seem to need the commentary; I…'

'I saw her change channels.'

'I know. She's always chasing the news. I just sit there and talk quietly, as I said. Every day for a week. Two hours today. I haven't got that much time – and tomorrow…' He looked suddenly broken and finished his whisky abruptly. 'Tomorrow will be awful.'

They looked at each other exhaustedly and Paul thought, he's as sick of this story as I am. Only a fortnight and it seems it will never end. Tomorrow will go on forever. He decided to try and sleep the whole of the following morning, to spare himself the wait.

'You knew her before, then? She went to mass and everything before?'

'Oh yes. Perhaps not well, she was always a little distant after her husband died, but she was pleasant enough, and generous. The boy was bright. Is bright. He was in my catechism class. Nothing unusual about either of them.' He hesitated. 'Now. Now I think she hates me.'

'How can you tell if she doesn't talk?'

'She looks at me. Not very often, but when she does. It's extremely unnerving, someone hating you, not opening their mouth. And yet I hope it *is* me; nothing worse.'

Paul looked at him. 'I could understand her hating God, if that's what you mean,' he said. 'It makes good sense to me. I can understand that even if I can't understand much else about her.'

'Can you?' said the priest.

'I think so,' said Paul, but he felt less sure.

They talked for a while longer until the fatigue was too much and Paul stood up, groggy with tiredness and whisky. In the fresh air on the doorstep he remembered the local newspaper piece and turned back to ask the priest if he had really said, 'Her faith and her love for Christ and the Holy Virgin is her greatest support; God will give her patience to endure.'

'Of course I didn't,' said the priest.

The morning papers carried a new picture and a reiterated threat. The boy's face was less blurred, and a new red weal sliced across one cheek. The eyes, still sunk in shadow, looked hopeless. Paul had failed to sleep in, and sat downstairs staring at the new picture. This time he didn't bother turning to his own piece at the back. The landlady hovered sympathetically with her opinion, but he didn't ask for it. After a while he went outside and walked down through the village. Ten o' clock mass was ringing from the big church on the square and he watched people filing self-consciously in. He might have been tempted to follow them, but remembered that his priest was not taking the service; they had drafted in a bishop as a mark of respect. Instead, he sat outside on the wall in weak sunlight. Some minutes later a sugary hymn tune floated out; he remembered it from somewhere, associated it with a string of meaningless complacencies about divine goodness. He sat, irritated but hypnotised, his eyes scanning the ground around him, registering tiny weeds and cracks in the stonework, until something – a cadence, a painful chord from the organ – triggered a clearer memory of that childhood fear.

He was in a church service, he thought with his grandmother, and he knew it was dark outside. He was fully aware that the occasion was exotic; at home, they did not go to church. The atmosphere, he supposed, was impressive, with singing and candles and massed murmured prayers, but all this was peripheral to the single image into which all his fear was collected: hanging on the wall ahead of him was a crude, bleeding heart, flickering in the candlelight. It was ghastly; he dreamed it for months afterwards. Worse than the assorted bloody crucifixions which he also remembered with distaste, this ludicrous, terrifying heart had fastened itself inside his head and hung there.

He realised now how much that image focused the unspoken bad feeling of that last summer in Brittany, the bitterness of an obscure war between his parents and his grandmother which he had sensed but never understood. He found himself wondering if his grandmother had indeed died the following year as he'd always thought, or whether there had been unreconciled summers before his father had gone away in a dark suit to the funeral and, sometime later, they had moved into a bigger flat. For some reason he found it impossible to remember anything specific about his grandmother, though he thought he could remember that she and he had got on well.

A cooler breeze moved him off the wall. He went down to the sea, back up to the cafe for a beer and a sandwich, and then back to his room where he lay on the bed for six or seven hours, dozing and smoking. Finally, he forced himself up, had a shower, and went back out into the village.

He made straight for the cafe and its television, half-aware that he was hoping for news of something happening; a capitulation, a reprieve. The place was full. No sign, of course, of his unreliable photographer, due down that evening to help capture the moment. Some of the men were friendlier now, and nodded to him, perhaps impressed to find that he knew no more than they did. He found himself an unobtrusive space and settled down to watch the screen. Nothing had happened; it was the same flow of pictures, solemn presenters, defensive ministers, shots of the middle east, helicopters. There were stills of the British soldier they had killed, and the same two or three images of the boy's pale face. His thoughts went to the priest and the mother, and he wondered whether, with hours to go, they were sitting in the kitchen in the blueish light of the screen, whether the priest's gentle discourse had finally worn her down.

Shortly before eleven he became unbearably restless and went out into the square to phone Sylvie. The phone rang and rang in their flat, and there was no reply. If she had gone out, she had forgotten to put the answerphone on. Hitting the buttons with increasing force he redialled once, then again, and then continuously for five minutes before slamming down the receiver and walking off into the night. Awash with self-pity, he decided to go to bed, a gesture he felt stood some chance of depriving him of his job, since his next piece, due in by 4am, was supposed to capture local reactions to whatever happened at midnight. Even as he started walking the doubts set in, and he begin to meander reluctantly back towards the cafe. Glancing across in the direction of the priest's house he saw it was dark. Just beyond the house, however, he was surprised to see lights in the little chapel of Our Lady. He must be there, he thought, praying. He would not disturb him, but he could go and look through a window and still get back in time. It would make a nice detail, the priest wrestling with his God.

The steps up the bank were crooked and slippery in the dark. The windows of the chapel shone golden. Because of the slope the windows were too high to see through, so he went into the porch. The door was ajar. He pushed at it very slowly and put his head round. The inside of the building was simple and hid nothing; it was empty. He slipped inside and looked towards the altar, radiant with clustered candles, lighting a wooden statue of the Virgin and Child. The gilt and pastel figures exuded the bland sweetness and docility of the hymn tune he had heard earlier; the baby was blond and curly. He thought of stern Byzantine Madonnas and their solemn precocious sons and felt the little chapel deserved better. But even kitsch by candlelight was mesmerising, and he sat down for a moment in the back pew, a moment of quiet before heading back out again to do his job.

The big door creaked again and a figure entered. Still half-expecting the priest, he was surprised to see a woman. She was carrying a little white bundle, and made towards the altar without noticing him. It was the hostage's mother. He felt afraid: partly trapped, partly curious, and pulled back into the shadows to watch.

Nothing that took place in that golden light could ever have felt like reality. The woman curtsied briefly to the statue, then bent her head for a moment in prayer. She lit another candle and found a place for it amongst the rest. Then she began to talk.

It was Breton, and quite meaningless to him except for the intonations, which sounded disconcertingly like normal conversation. Neither ritual nor plea, it sounded calm and reasonable, like an explanation. Paul watched her, a small strong figure in a darkish coat and headscarf; he caught glimpses of her face as she looked up into the pink and white smile of Mary. Only the arms, which held the white bundle tightly, suggested strain. After a minute or so the voice began to change; the words came quicker and louder. He had a sense of cajolement and anger, at once persuasive and bitter. He felt a flicker of the childhood fear. He was afraid she would let go entirely, give herself up to hysteria; but at the same time he couldn't resist a growing excitement at this spectacular reaction from the woman whose silence and deadened stare had left him lost for words. It was then he remembered the camera.

It had not been part of his brief to do pictures. But he knew perfectly well how often the best shots were unplanned, fortuitous; he knew how much money a really emotive picture could make. His camera was a decent one, for its size; he'd taken good shots in the past.

She was not crying yet, but had definitely reached despair. The voice filled the chapel. She still had her back to him, was still clutching the bundle; he slid the camera out of his pocket and began fiddling with the flash and the lens, sitting as still as possible. He lifted it experimentally to his eye, but the image was disappointing; he would have to wait for a more dramatic gesture.

Another change of key. Calmer now, but perhaps, he thought, closer to tears. She moved at last, unrolling her white bundle on the altar. It was a woollen shawl. Paul stood up to see better, camera ready. She patted it flat and then turned back to the statue. Mary's tender inclined face smiled down at her like a doll. Before Paul could even begin to realise what was happening the woman had climbed awkwardly up onto the dais and reached out for the little Christ. There was a grotesque moment of pushing and pulling as the child came free and the woman almost fell backwards, stumbling off the dais. Paul froze with shock as she laid the little statue on its back on the white shawl and wrapped its stiff limbs with care. She stood again in front of the Virgin, said something, and bowed her head; then she turned to leave. He tried to lift the camera, but couldn't, and did not try again.

As she came up the aisle he pressed himself further into the shadows, his right arm with the camera hanging uselessly at his side. He saw how naturally, how protectively, she held the bundled wooden child. The door creaked and she was gone. In fear and distress he took a few steps forward towards the candles and their unreal haze. The gilded Madonna shone as brightly as ever, smiling her tenderness into a new and awful space.

Centaur

It must be thirty years since I last saw my hands on a steering wheel. Positioned carefully at ten to two, as originally instructed. I sit up straight and look at them, these hands that are not my hands, all gnarled and wrinkled and flecked with brown smudges. You would not trust these hands to hold her steady, or take a bend; you would not relax if one of these hands lifted nonchalantly to point out a red kite, or jab for a radio station, or reach for a paper cup. These hands are hanging on for dear life.

Not that we are going anywhere. No wheels. Not much chassis. And if, which I doubt, there is still an engine trapped in the twisted bonnet it will be mostly powdered rust. It is surprising to find the seat and the steering wheel so much their old selves. Perhaps tractors hang on to their identity for longer. I wonder if this was a Ferguson, a grey one, like ours.

How astonishing, though, to find it. That there could be anything within our ten-mile radius to recover after so long, when all we have done for the last fifteen years is walk and walk and forage every inch. I'm glad there's so little of it left, I do not want to dismantle it. I said I'd bring wood and I will bring wood. Leave it here hidden until someone younger and harder comes along.

Picasso turned bicycles into bulls. This beast is as skeletal, and nearly as mythical. I don't feel inclined to get off just yet, though it is cold, February cold, with the wind that carries the starlings and that pale light which is unnerving me as ever. I watch my strange hands get colder.

You grandfather was a centaur: a lovely man. For the first year of our acquaintance, after I came to the village school, all I ever saw of him was in lanes, in passing; he used to raise a courteous hand, and smile. If we met head to head he would back, swiftly, confidently, the way an iceskater can reverse with barely a flick of the hips, perfectly following the narrow line of the road, whatever he was driving. I never got the hang of that. We all had wheels, back then, but not all of us were born to it, brought up to it, like the boys in the village, who drove little quads at five, and became fully themselves, their four-wheeled selves, at puberty in beaten-up fiestas and second-best tractors. It was normal, then, to drive a hundred yards to a neighbour's house. Normal to run down to the coast for a bottle of milk or a newspaper; to crawl round the village delivering Christmas cards. Pretty well all the farm work was on wheels: tractors, landrovers and diggers, trucks, quads, funny little mules like golf buggies. Shepherds circled the hills in shiny pick-ups. Sheep came running to the sound of a thick fist smashed down, again and again, on the horn.

The green or muddy tracks you run and ride along were hedged and tarmacked; hardly smooth at the very best of times, but drivable, except in the snow, which came like a premonition of the quality of future silences, but which did not, in the beginning, come every year. There was, just like in the stories, a friendly postman in a red van; there were endless white-van delivery men, usually from Birmingham, usually lost, huge and tottering haylorries, a ramshackle school bus, even a proper bus to town. And three or four times a year everyone would get up in the middle of the night, and wake small children, and bring them down huddled in their dressing gowns to watch the Rally. They waited, and waited. Eventually out of the dark would come the vicious whine of an engine curving down the hill, then a brief gap in the noise, and then the roar and flash as it tore past. Like giant angry wasps, but singly, not swarming, their attacks uncomfortably spaced apart. Your grandfather always got up with the children. I always stayed in bed and braced myself for the noise of a car losing control, smashing the gate, the wall, my children. The headlights strafed our room through the thin curtains; in the morning people discussed the skid marks on the road.

The first time I saw him properly without wheels, up on the stage in chapel at the village eisteddfod, squashed onto a little chair with my class of serious-eyed children, I fell in love with him. He looked like Gulliver, absurd and gentle, directing each child forward to say their piece; I went through agonies for every one. A tatty poster behind him said *Myfi Yw'r Atgyfodiad*, I Am the Resurrection, and when, surprisingly, he grinned at me across the hall, across the heads of his tribe, I thought yes, why not. And I taught in that school until they closed it down around us, when, they said, the roads were too bad for the buses, and they had no more money for anything out of town, it was all going on flood defences at that time. But we managed the route for several more years after that, in and out, though you got to think twice about doing it often, as the potholes deepened and the ice clawed up more of the tarmac every winter.

I try to unclamp my hands from the steering-wheel but they feel locked. I can hear the squeal of starlings in the thin trees around me. I know I should try harder, I know how stiff my legs will be. It was a mistake to stop walking. The noise the birds make is like something whistling, boiling, damn them, it is a most unnatural sound. When the rains started we moved out of the schoolhouse up to his brother's, and the two of them spent much of their time adapting vehicles for the whole village. Thanks to them most people round here were already on vegetable oil by the time the diesel ran out. They created new, bizarre, hybrid vehicles out of pieces of old ones as they fell apart. We were still driving two years into the Emergency, though as the sea ate into the coast road, and town was flooded from both sides, we did not drive far. When the deadlines came several families who had hung on decided to leave; your uncle Ifan left then too, to help with the relocation of the town. But there were plenty who didn't. Your mother and I set up a little school in the kitchen, there were still enough village children then for a proper class. We sang, we recited, and we began teaching them to walk and forage. He started to fail around then; small things, I noticed them, but he wouldn't talk about it, he was stubborn like that.

The squealing is disturbing, but even stranger is the noise they make as they take off, a kind of *thwup*, like canvas pulled taut or caught in a gust. I said I'd bring wood. I should make an effort now, I've been here long enough for birds and animals to start ignoring me, rabbits, squirrels, magpies, a wren. I think about my feet, wrapped in wool and stuffed into boots, but I can't feel them; my hips I can feel, though, that usual ache. If we had gone then, when there were still hospitals, and, if not for cures, extraordinary possibilities. Stubborn man. I think that must be snowdrops, that bright patch up ahead, though I can't see terribly well these days; it could be water, in among the birches and alders. I expect there's some decent wood in there too, since no one else can have been this way for some time. If we had gone then, when there were still hospitals. I said, didn't I, that I'd bring wood, but you'll have to get it yourselves, won't you, now; I expect there's some good stuff in among the trees up ahead.

I remember a particular tree at the edge of the village, where the lane turned down. A big grey rowan. This time of year, this terrible pale light, and we were walking, slowly was all he could manage by then – no wheels, see – and as we came round the corner this tree was full of starlings. The way it held them all, one on every twig, it looked like a black magnolia, thick with black buds. We knew by then what was going to happen, but he said look at that now, *drycha draw fanna*, and when I said I was frightened he just laughed, he said there was no need.

Fish

The fish, we decide, are getting to us. You should write and tell him, I say, and she laughs with wicked pleasure at the thought.

Dear Husband
No
Beloved partner…
Ha, ha.
Ok. Dear Richard.

You don't really need the dear I think uncharitably, but clamp my teeth firmly together this time, as I have failed to do so many times before.

Dear Richard,
I sometimes find it hard to cope. Especially with the fish.
Your everloving wife
Louise.

It might make him think, I say. It would give you a place to start.
There are so many places I could start, she says, why pick on the poor fish?

Because like you they are always in the kitchen. No. That's not fair. You are often in the park, pushing the middle one, holding the baby one, calling out to the older one encouragingly, mostly. And you are sometimes on the beach, huddled at the top out of the wind, supervising the catastrophic collapse of two ice creams onto the big grey pebbles. And you are sometimes, most days in fact, to be found pounding your beat between school and home and nursery, in rain that on a bad day comes down like sticks and stones. You won't catch fish doing that. But we both of us do our time in our kitchens, back and forth, over and over, moving through the same tracks in air that must be full of us, our breath, our scent of skin and babies.

Green tea with jasmine. Dark, dark chocolate, a small square each. And I don't have to tell her why the fish because my youngest has wet himself, again, and I go out scolding, rummaging for little pants in my hopelessly flung-together hessian bag. She is better prepared than I am, mostly.

But absolutely the fish, I think. A big, huge tankful on the worktop, and what a lovely idea, the flick and glimmer of them back and forth, an accompaniment, barely acknowledged, to our own backs and forths. Bought for children and tended by mothers all over the land. How many of us, I wonder, stop in their air tracks in moments of complete distraction and stare into the tank? Briefly pulled into the fishworld, its pebbles and weed, and briefly lost in there with the fish who slip in and out of view, or hang quietly behind twisted wood.

She settles back on the low sofa and clamps the baby on for a feed so I take over the supervision of pitta bread in the toaster and pick over her fridge, cleaner than mine, for hummus, philadelphia, cucumber, ham, olives. She tells me about an article she has read on David Jones; you should publish your thesis, I say, not for the first time. She wrinkles her nose at me. Then I tell her about having lunch with an archivist up at the library who is cataloguing the contents of Edward Thomas' last diary; he told me that you can see the ripple marks on the paper from the shock of that last shell. A brutal folding of the air around him, like stamping on a tin can.

The fish, though. We don't often stop to watch them; they are mostly sensed peripherally, on our way to somewhere else, let's say the sink. Peripheral vision is what you use when you're driving; especially when you do the same bit of road every day, sometimes twice. Eyes on the grey ribbon but you absorb the differences on either side without thinking: the height of the hedges, the curved lines of grass in the field cut for silage. Snowdrops primroses bluebells stitchwort red campion, in that order; a random crisp packet, a dead badger. Me anyway, not her, since she doesn't drive. I think that might be his fault, too; at least that's how I interpret it, and he did once say, to my face, to my eternal astonishment, that he didn't marry her because he thought she would ever *drive* and that she was quite the wrong person to put behind the wheel of a car. To my face.

It is exactly the same kind of vision which allows you to be acutely aware of the fish. To move with a plateful of pitta bread, as I do now, from toaster to table, stepping over crayons and cars and calling them in from the front room to come and sit up without a sideways glance. If this were my kitchen I would know exactly what stage of the cycle we were at, how far into the slow greening of the glass, the thickening of slime around the filter, the gradual poisoning of the water. I would know from the way they moved, from the level they hang, lethargic or lively, just how uncomfortable I should be feeling. It builds up, over five or six or weeks, depending on the weather.

Well this is chaos, as ever. Two fighting, one crying about something else entirely, one tucking in blithely oblivious. I move in to break up the fight. She gently unclamps the blissed-out baby and lowers him into the buggy by the window, holding her breath, hoping he won't wake. He doesn't. She deals with the crying one, and then we hover round the table, making encouraging noises and spreading cheese; diving in like gannets on the olives once in a while. She has that grace about her.

More tea? I ask.
Mmm. I'll make it.
What next? I've got an hour.
Too cold for the park? This wind.
This rain. Oh no, it's stopped. But still. Beach?
Not sure I'm strong enough. They're quite happy playing here.

And I'm tired, she says, going back to the sofa with her hands cradled round her mug, I'm tired in my bones and my head. My eyes are too tired to read. My ears are too tired to listen. I have to remember to put the bins out tonight and get enough wood in for a fire that I will be too tired to sit by, and put three small children to bed, one after the other, as I've done for five weeks now and counting, and probably fall asleep in the process and wake up in my clothes feeling…

When is he back?
God knows, and when he's back he works so late it comes to the same thing.
I know, I say. I really do: at least, I can imagine it. I couldn't manage the way you do, not for more than a couple of nights and even then I'm shouting blue murder at them by day three.
Right inside my bones, she says. Fatigue.

I think of her lying in bed crying, with the fatigue latching onto every cell in her bones, her dancer's bones, like the inverse of osteoporosis, transforming them into something not light and brittle but too heavy to bear. The same with her thoughts, her bright mind, all the quick pathways furred up with exhaustion.

Like trying to think through soup, I say.
I should make more soup, she says dreamily. They eat that.
Best way of getting vegetables…
…into them, I know.

One of mine comes in and gives me an unscripted kiss on the arm and goes out again looking important and mysterious. We laugh.

You're right about the fish, she says.
I know I am.

I actually lost one a couple of weeks ago but I'm not confessing to it. It happened fast. One day, from nowhere, it had developed horrible popping eyes and sank to a couple of inches above the bottom of the tank and hung there. Water quality, it said accusingly on the web, but no amount of clean water could stop the rot. I put it in its own pyrex bowl, a tiny glass leperhouse, and hid it from the kids. It took far too long to die, and fell apart grotesquely when I fished it out to dispose of; it must have been half rotted-through before it had even stopped living. This is not something you tell people. But suppose I multiply my own circle of friends by, say, a mere million, that adds up, I feel, to a lot of mothers quietly carrying round these grisly little moments of failure.

The answer – and this, at the moment, seems to be the answer to everything – is to clean regularly. Different people do it in different ways, but I always transfer the fish to a bowl, chasing them around the tank with a little net, and hoik them out wriggling, one at a time, two if you're lucky. I keep about half the old water, which I believe is full of good bacteria, and fetch cold fresh water from the little stream down the side of the house. I clean the green slime off everything, the weirdly furred-up bits of wood, the darkened pebbles, even the gravel. I scrape it off the glass, degunk the filter. It takes a long time and once I start that's it, I never rush it, and I never stop in the middle of the cleaning to do something else, however much hell breaks loose around me; which must make it almost unique amongst household tasks. The reward: bright pebbles, quick fish, a cleansed and righteous soul.

I clear up the plates. Today, I sense, is not a day for fighting talk, for one of my harangues: rise up, girl, do something write something join a class learn to drive (yes *drive*, ha!) take control walk out get a part-time job learn a language make him do a day a week, just one. What must I sound like, half the time. No, we're both mid-week November weary, and happy enough to keep making tea and manage the conflicts and crises that break out like little whirlpools in the sea of children around us. Occasionally we throw out the beginnings of a conversation across the room, about books or things that matter from our childhood, and watch as their strands get pulled down into the little vortices, unravelled, shredded. Much later, when she has left for another country, I will think that perhaps the shipwrecked quality of our conversations makes them more significant. Now I can't forget how she said she loved having her nails cut, because then, for half an hour or so, she had her mother all to herself.

She uncurls from the sofa and starts washing up. I find a tea towel and come over to dry, picking mugs and plates off the stainless-steel drainer. She looks at the silver space I'm making and gives a little shiver, a kind of shrug.

I came down one morning, she says, and found one of the small fish on the draining board, there, it must have flipped itself out all that way, it was twisted, tiny, with its mouth open.

No, I say, don't tell me. I don't want to know.

Fish

There is a noise from the pram, the preliminary half-coughing *ack-ack-ack* before the first real lungful of yell. She gets to him first, lifts him nuzzling into her neck. I finish clearing the table, and look with some envy at the highchair, which is implausibly clean and bright. How do you get it so clean, I say, ours is always covered in weetabix and dried yoghurt.

She looks at me across the room, helpless, beautiful, defiant. Wry.
It's what I do, she says.

Lake Story

Rhag bod annwyd ar fy mab	If my son should find it cold
Rhoddwch arno gôb ei dad.	Wrap him in his father's coat
Rhag bod annwyd ar liw'r can	If the fair one feels the cold
Rhoddwch arni bais ei mam.	Wrap her in my petticoat.

When the levels rise the plants around the edge find themselves under water. Tiny yellow four-petalled tormentil. Buttercups and rusty sphagnum moss and even the reeds, even the grass. And they do look strange held there, more significant somehow, breathing in the wrong element for a while at least, until the levels drop again and release them. The space she inhabits works something like that. There are days driving home when I can tell our village has gone under. Days when it spills down from the lake up on the hill, and floods over the cattlegrids so that you pass into it about halfway up the back lane. The familiar skyline expresses it too, but really it is the quality of the air that changes. There are days when it happens, days when it doesn't. It may be something to do with the light.

The children, hers and mine, are down by the edge of the lake, and the older ones are lunging optimistically with nets and the smaller ones are playing a game that involves jumping off stones and frightening the shoals of tiny bright fish out of their senses, and although it is early afternoon on the hottest day of the year so far, my feet are grey and cold from standing in the lake and I have withdrawn to a dryish hummock of grass to try and remove my boots which are suddenly unbearable. I know I am keeping a perfectly adequate half an eye on them, but half is clearly not enough as she appears from somewhere and hovers around making concerned noises; it's mine she's worried about, as ever. I tell her not to be. I tell her to come and sit down and stop being so restless; the kids, I say, are all right.

And in truth it is one of those days when I feel gratified and triumphant at having engineered a perfect childhood moment. Look, not a screen in sight, not even a phone, there being no signal, and all electronic equipment stashed safe in a rucksack perched on a stone wall, and everyone getting on a treat – adding hers, that much older, to mine, always did result in outbreaks of harmony. Look at that, I say, and then, entirely without irony: don't you wish we had a camera?

Then she does settle at last and I grin at her and say if I'd known you were joining us I'd have packed a nice bottle of white. Another time, she says. I'll come up on my own one evening perhaps, I say, and bring one then. I don't drink much now, she says. Of course she doesn't.

Springwater?

Raindrops, she says, and/or dew.

Et avec ça?

Oh, she says, vaguely, just scraps and strands. Lichen, sorrel, new hawthorn leaves, and the inevitable *llus bach duon*.

Bilberries. And there was me blaming the sheep.

All the smart Cardiff folks, I said, at your funeral, I don't know what they made of the bilberry-picking after the fourth or fifth mention; they must think, us being so far from Tescos and all, that we live from hand to mouth up here, foraging; they must think the whole tribe's survival depends on it.

It does, in a way, she says, after some consideration.

Rowan berries? I ask quickly.

She pulls a face. Sour, but yes in small doses. What else do I like now? Watermint, honeysuckle, cake.

Cake?

Even in death, she says enigmatically, there is cake.

We were proud as queens, I say, that day at the summer fête, do you remember, manning the cake stall…?

Womanning the cake stall, she says, wrinkling her nose.

Indeed. I made at least five myself, though I can't rememember what they all were, apple I expect, and lemon, and a bara brith, the usual. And you would have done *teisen lap* and that plain one the boys like with chocolate on top.

There must have been more, she says.

There were, it was epic.

Homeric.

Like the Tractor Run this year. When they massed up here on the hill against the skyline with the whole of the bay before them. From all over the county they came. That really was the stuff of epic; there should have been someone standing up at Hafod Ithel twanging a traditional three-stringed instrument and calling them in: naming each and every one as they came trundling over the hill in their ancient glory and reciting their various virtues – oh, but you missed them, you were gone by then.

Not really, she says mildly. Go and rescue that child.

I clamber off my tussock and pick my way clumsily across the boggy land back down to the shingle beach of the lake, but by the time I get there the child has been picked up and comforted by an older one, one of hers.

You see, I say, they self-regulate.

Needs a dry top, she says, he'll catch cold.

All the Souls

Woman it is the hottest day of the year and he's more likely to catch an octopus than a cold, but I know from your expression how worried you get about this, how deeply anxious it makes you to think that any of them might ever be cold, and I stumble over to the rucksacks, grazing my legs gently on nettles, and pull out an oversize t-shirt with which I manage to bag him from behind, like a little fish. *Twtyn*, she says tenderly.

In a matter of seconds, I say very gravely, that t-shirt will be soaking wet.

I find a flattish rock on the slope above the nettles and take in a different view of the lake, the ruined folly in the far reeds, the collapsed cottages, the beeches that used to be somebody's hedge now a row of grey-limbed giants; one of them housing a raggedy nest, a buzzard or a kite, I can't remember, her eldest knows which. An RAF jet smashes through the lot, leaves us quivering.

Uwch llonyddwch... I quote wryly, and scramble down to reassure the most frightened, and to say something flattening to one of the older ones who is unashamedly impressed, and then I stand in the shallow water and wait for the world to subside, for the lake to stop shivering. When I can see the underwater plants and the flash of a stickleback I go back up to my rock and hope that she will come back.

I pick up a sharp slate and pretend to feel its edge. Thought I might go up and deface the Poets' Stone in your honour, I say loudly, you're one of them now aren't you, *Beirdd y Mynydd*, you and Beti both:

I gofio'r gwŷr – (*a'r gwragedd!!*)
Fu'n nyddu llên   [In memory of the men (*and the women!!*)
                                  who crafted verse
Uwch llonyddwch   above the tranquility
Llyn ....   of Lake....]

Another plane screams through, but this time I don't go back down: see, how quickly they get used to it, even the little ones, a smile is enough this time.

Do they stick together? I wonder. The poets, I mean.

They do, she says, sitting down on the turfy grazed patch beside me.

Cliquey?

Well; you know.

Are they here too? I ask. It's always only you.

Matter of time, matter of perspective, she says. But it's busy enough, yes. Put your foot on my foot if you want to see.

My feet are still cold but they have a bit more life in them by now and I stretch out a tentative leg in wet, rolled-up jeans towards her. She is sitting with her arms wrapped round her knees, looking like a girl. Her hair shines copper. There are tiny flecks of paint on her forearms. I can't feel her foot of course, but I feel a lurch, like being downstairs on a big ferry, and then I start to see various groups of people walking around the lake. They are blurry, and somehow faded, but I can see them, mostly wearing black, with smudges of white shirts, white collars, white aprons. Calvinist revivalists, farmers, labourers, talking away quietly, absorbed in their groups. I think I see Beti, walking more easily than she has done for years, and probably, from the look of her at this distance, telling jokes. And further up there are two or three old-fashioned-looking children, bizarrely pulling a sledge through the reeds. I take my foot away quickly then as a forgotten local half-story surfaces; I don't want to see the children with their sledge.

A small cloud briefly turns the lake a steely grey. I try to describe how some days it feels as if the village is flooded with neither light nor water, and she nods.

I get past the grids on those days, she says.

The cattlegrids?

Mm. Supposed to keep us to the uplands. Can't touch the metal. But I come and go a lot, really, especially on those days.

I know you do, I say.

Then I see that the sun has slipped, and that there is a haze coming slowly in from the sea. It will be a trek back down the hill with this lot. I can see that the smallest one has had enough, and is bravely making his way towards me, struggling for balance over the mounds of moss and reeds.

Aros funud! I call, and in a single predictable movement he looks up to my voice and falls over on his face at the edge of the spreading stream, where the peat is rich and black and the water is like stewed tea. She is already bending over him, all helpless concern: *o twtyn*, she says, *o cariad bach*. And I heave him upright and pull his sopping t-shirt up over his head and wipe the worst of the peat off his face, and laugh at how yellow he is already, all over, a little Tollund Man, perfectly preserved.

Dewch, you lot; ni'n mynd! They gather strewn clothing, buckets, nets. I strip the little peaty one and find the last dry t-shirt, which comes down to his knees, and carry him laboriously up to the road where I set him down on his feet and kiss him, and go down to collect a forgotten bucket and help the other two smaller ones, and chivvy the rest. *Dewch ymlaen.* She stands patiently on guard up on the road but she is stooping now and I can tell she's starting to fret.

I can manage, I say, don't worry, they'll be home soon, and dry and fed. Look how strong they are, how full of energy. It's a lovely evening. They'll be fine. Come on, now, don't fuss.

But there is a flicker of panic about her now, and I can hear her insisting, not to me, or to anyone else, but over and over, how cold it is, how they need their fleeces, to make sure they wear them, *bydden nhw'n oer ac yn wlyb*. She isn't thinking about the little ones.

They're not cold, I say. Look at them. They know when they're cold. And you know that by now I can't make them any more than you can, none of us can, now come on, they'll be fine, they've had a lovely day, let them go, they'll be home and dry in no time.

But they need…

I summon all my strength to be firm with her.

It's getting late, I say. Let me deal with this lot. You go and call your cattle in.

And she tears herself away at last to look anxiously around the slopes.

God yes, she says. There's always something.

And she heads off through the heather and the gorse for the higher ground, calling in a language I don't understand.

I turn towards the children straggled out along the narrow mountain road, and consider the various permutations for piggy-backs. The mist will meet us about halfway down the hill, I think, but that's fine, we still have plenty of time. We go very slowly, as if exhausted, like explorers in a strange land. As we reach the crest a line of calling geese fly over us, heading back towards the lake.

Acknowledgements

'The Collectors' was written with the help of a bursary from the Academi; I am very grateful indeed for the time it bought, and the motivation it provided. Thanks too, to Gwen Davies for encouraging me to get a collection together, to Francesca Rhydderch for renewing wavering resolve, and to Penny Thomas at Seren for her thoughtful and tactful editing.

'The Collectors' grew out of earlier work on nineteenth-century Breton popular traditions; 'Z' and Le Coadic are loosely based on historical characters, but (as far as I know) never met. I would like to thank Donatien Laurent for permission to use fragments of the 'Skolan' ballad he collected, and also, many years ago, for telling me the story reprised in 'Warrior'; Éva Guillorel kindly looked over my Breton.

Love and thanks as ever to all my family, especially David, my most encouraging reader.

'Absolution' appeared in the collection edited by Gwen Davies, *Sing Sorrow, Sorrow* (Seren, 2010); 'Lake Story' appeared in the *New Welsh Review* 99 (Spring, 2012).

SEREN

Well chosen words

Seren is an independent publisher with a wide-ranging list which includes poetry, fiction, biography, art, translation, criticism and history. Many of our books and authors have been shortlisted for – or won – major literary prizes, among them the Costa Award, the Man Booker, Forward Prize, and TS Eliot Prize.

At the heart of our list is a good story told well or an idea or history presented interestingly or provocatively. We're international in authorship and readership though our roots are here in Wales (Seren means Star in Welsh), where we prove that writers from a small country with an intricate culture have a worldwide relevance.

Our aim is to publish work of the highest literary and artistic merit that also succeeds commercially in a competitive, fast changing environment. You can help us achieve this goal by reading more of our books – available from all good bookshops and increasingly as e-books. You can also buy them at 20% discount from our website, and get monthly updates about forthcoming titles, readings, launches and other news about Seren and the authors we publish.

www.serenbooks.com